MARRIED BY WAR

SARAH K. L. WILSON

SPARKFLIGHT BOOKS

HALDUR OAKENSEN

Snow squeaks as I adjust my weight on feet so frozen that they could be blocks of dead oak and not living human appendages. I grimace at the sound – faint as it is – and my breath huffs to mingle with Hessa's doggy gusts. We two are one in this moment – bound by ties of love and loyalty but also in the need to keep silent and wait.

I ease my hand on her head in a moment of shared comfort, though her brown eyes are bright with anticipation and her tongue lolls with excitement. For me, the only feeling inside is fear. Whatever glamour dazzles my eyes and fills my waking days with nightmares does not affect her. She hunts by scent and feel, a living spirit greater than her doggy body manifests. I, human as I am, must hunt with murky senses – a nose that tells me nothing of my opponent unless he sets the trees ablaze, ears and eyes deadened by my weak mortal flesh.

The sound of a twig snapping – not from behind where our pickets lie, but from in front – sends an echo of movement down our line. My breath hitches, tight on the cold air, tighter on the fear I keep gripped down against my breastbone. There's something about a group of warriors that makes them one entity in the fight. Individual but not. More aligned even, than a murder of crows or a pack of wolves. We are one in spirit, for all of us streak like arrows toward one target.

Today's target is an ambush.

Hands shift their grip on weapons – even mine on this sword I've come to both love and hate. My salvation and my damnation, an extension of my violent self.

Their arrival is not quiet. Even the fae, magical as they are, cannot change the nature of snow when the cold descends long and brutal on the earth and rules us harder than tyrants. It announces them as easily as a trumpet, and I bite the inside of my lip as I flash my hand signals to the men on either side of me.

They've taken the bait. They'll be amongst us soon. Now is the moment to hold our nerve and be ready.

Answering signals rippled down to meet me.

Every man knows his job. Every boy, too, and there are too many of those. This war has gone too long. We're left now with boys and old men. A man in his prime still living is such an oddity that some of the men make sacred signs when they catch sight of one.

I'm one of the boys lifted to rank too soon. Barely twenty. Only just a man. My father and brothers cut down in the past twenty moons and carved away until I'm the last to bear the name and standard. Me and Hessa. The only ones left who once lived on Castle Tor.

I can hear the voices of my enemies now. It's a shock every time.

Before we fight, we see them as men – or as close to men as fae can be, with their pointed ears, and wings, and horned heads. As close to men as fae can be while riding elk, or big cats, and fighting with lightning strikes as often as with blade or staff.

The moment we charge them, they'll shift to monsters of shadow and the ripping horrors of hell unfolded.

But for this one painful moment, we see them enter our trap looking not entirely unlike us. As if they have hearts that beat. As if they have hearts that love. Just like us.

I wrap up these thoughts and bind them down with my terror. No room for them here. No place for them.

Our quarry is spread out along the snow-packed trail. They follow in each other's paths like yellow ducklings following the mother.

I bite the inside of my cheek until it bleeds, until I remember that there's no room for anything but the work at hand. And then I chop my hand through the air, and we charge.

Hessa, too. I dare not worry for her. Her doggy instincts will keep her safe. They always do.

"For the valor of the Blue Eagle! The Blue Eagle!" someone screams down the line.

"The Blue Eagle!" The cry is taken up around me.

I save my breath, plunging forward as the world transforms from bright white snow and charcoal branches to a howling mass of black smoky creatures with red fires for eyes and mouths, their faces distended and drawn out until they look more like billows of smoke come alive to attack us than like the pretty golden-haired men in bright armor that I saw from my hiding place.

I swing my sword and slice at one, and then quickly turn the motion and hack to the other side. Strike, strike, advance. Strike, strike, advance. Just like the training yard. Just like practice. I must ignore how they howl in my mind. I must ignore how they seem to find my every evil thought and wish and bring it to the front of my consciousness and whip me with them. My own heart accuses me and tells me to surrender and die.

I must not agree.

Strike, strike, advance.

Hessa howls as her teeth sink into the shadow figure I fight.

Strike, strike – he falls, morphing back into a man-like shape, his golden hair spilling around him in the snow, his bright armor frosted at the edges with the last heat of his life, his red, red blood staining snow and ice around him.

And I have no time to stop. I spin to the next.

Gragor shouts from beside me, his throat caught in a shadow hand. I spin and plunge my blade into the shadow. Gragor drops into a defensive stance and strikes out in a slash, too tough to break at the attack, despite his willow-fresh fourteen years.

Our shadow enemy crumples into a dead fae adorned with antlers like a deer's. He'd be beautiful if his life hadn't spilled out, stunning if he hadn't been a demon creature a moment ago.

I step over his corpse, binding any pity I feel down to that place where the other things are trapped in close to my spine, behind my breastbone.

And my sword works and works as I spin and weave and dance the old dance of death I've been trained for. I take no pleasure in violence. Those who live by the sword die by the sword. I don't think I'll hate the dying any worse than I hate the living.

Fergan flicks fingers at me from down the line. I look to the right and left quickly.

Our ambush has been successful. We huff together in the cold – tattered, bloody, dirty, and too thin. We stand over the dead like gaunt coyotes over dead songbirds. Not enough meal to feed us. Winning and losing all at once.

I want to sink to the ground and feel it all. But I won't. I won't.

Hessa slides her head against my leg, and I let myself put a trembling hand on her head. I can't afford weakness, but maybe I can indulge in this one small display. Her muzzle is red with blood. She favors one paw. I'll have to check it.

"We got them, Haldur!" Gragor laughs from beside me.

He either does not let himself care or does not let himself notice how many of ours are strewn among our enemies. There's Old Brathur with a cut throat, eyes empty as his skin turns white. There's Jehn the carver's youngest son. His face is purple, eyes bulging. Gragor would have died just like that if I hadn't noticed him. I swallow down bile.

"We killed them all and their hellspawn mounts!" Gragor cheers.

I clap him on the shoulder with a grunt. I don't want to see the day his enthusiasm rots to bitterness. Although it would be nice if he lived that long.

Fergan flicks his fingers again. He's my second. He's been busy counting. We lost fourteen to the sixteen we pulled down. Only surprise and greater numbers bought us that much advantage. Only war would consider that a victory.

I want to curse.

I don't. I've learned that words can only hurt. I try to avoid them as much as I can.

Trellan jogs up, his worn coat flapping in the wind. It was his brother's and Henta was twice as wide in the shoulders before he was gutted by a fae monster.

"Message," he gasps. "We're to return to camp fast as we can."

I nod and grunt my understanding, fingers flicking to Fergan. It's not what we expected and in war, surprises are never good.

2

HALDUR OAKENSEN

I don't have time to do more than carry our dead to the pyres and clean my blade before we have more messengers breathing down our necks.

"Hurry," they say.

"You're needed, Sir Oakensen," they say.

"The king has asked for you by name," they say.

I answer them with dour looks and nods and grunts when I must. The king has only asked for the Oakensen name because of my father and brothers. He asks for it because he remembers it in an army of people he no longer knows, gutted of nobility and pride. Strangers dragged out from croft and keep, to fight in this endless, hopeless war.

And they only call me Sir because my father was a knight and the king's hasty signature upon his death and the deaths of my brothers – all in the same battle – left him desperate to fill the role. Blood, it seems, trumps experience.

But I go with them.

What else would I do?

I pause long enough to find a little rabbit jerky for Hessa. She's owed that. She wags her tail and twitches her soft eyebrows at me. Anyone who says dogs don't know human emotion has never met a Hessa dog. I don't speak to her except to touch her head, and that's all she needs to stay with Fergan and wait for me.

"Going up to the Command tent?" he asks me quietly when I leave Hessa with him. Fergan ought to be enjoying his dotage carving wooden animals for children and offering sage advice to me about how to court a lady, or how to settle a dispute. Instead, his old bones must fight with us on this field of madness.

"Mm," I agree.

"If there is any chance of it, negotiate hot food for the men. It's been a sevenday since we've seen so much as soup," he says, as if I don't know. As if my own belly is not an aching emptiness within me. But hope burns at the back of his eyes.

I can't tell those eyes that I won't ask. They're so hollow. His cheeks, likewise, are sunken. I swallow down words of hope and worry. There's no word that can bring the comfort he needs – the comfort any of them need.

A quick glance over the poor souls in my keeping, and I see his hopeful gaze echoed from eye to eye as they look at me. I'm their representative before the king. The last knight of Castle Tor. I'll do what I can for them as long as I'm alive to do it. I clench a fist as I renew that vow in the deepest part of my heart.

Briskly, I nod my farewell to them and follow the

latest messenger, a boy of perhaps eight summers. He shouldn't be here. He should be home with his mother. Perhaps he no longer has one.

I follow his impatient steps. I don't like how thin he is. Someone should be feeding him. Someone should be feeding all of them.

I wipe my face with a palm, trying to scrub away worry, and then grimace. My hand is dirty. I'd forgotten. Likely, I've made myself more disreputable-looking than I already am.

We move from the sprawling edge of the camp nearest the battlegrounds and inward toward the main body of the army. I can smell tension here. Muscles bunched, heads ducked, whispers, and sideways looks.

"What's happened?" I ask the boy, but he doesn't answer, and I don't stop to ask someone else. When I get there, I will find out. Perhaps an important knight has fallen – or a lord. I think we still have some of those. Perhaps we've lost an entire band. God forbid, we may have lost the king.

I quicken my pace, still slower than the boy. He darts ahead like an eager puppy. Like Hessa when she was small.

Our king has positioned his command tent on a hill a little back from the sprawling fires of his army. We hustle up the bare rocks past the rings of soldiers keeping guard. Just a glance at the nearest one makes him grip his polearm tighter. They're on edge. My presence shouldn't spook them, but it does.

They take one look at my tabard, at the blue eagle sigil on the breast, and they let me through. Some look away or meet my eyes with pity. They all know who I am, though I know none of them. They're the king's vassals, not mine. I don't owe them my blood and days. Those are for the poor ragged skeletons I left with Hessa.

Not a single soldier here in the main camp is at rest. None are eating, or patching gear, or sharpening blades. I clench my jaw. Something bad is happening. No one is this tense for good news.

I'm almost at the command tent before I realize what is different. It's too bright. And who are those shadows on the other side of the hill? Is that a stag that I see?

I place a heavy hand on the messenger boy's shoulder, and he pauses, looking up at me with fear in his eyes. I'm rough with battle and though I'm not yet filled in with a man's full muscle, it's enough to give a boy pause.

"There are visitors," I say, and his eyes widen. I have spoken mildly. If you must speak, you should keep your words gentle on the ears of those who hear them.

"Yes, Sir Oakensen."

"Fae?" I press quietly.

"Yes, noble Sir."

"Numbers?"

"A dozen," a voice from beside us says. It's one of the King's vassals. He's brandishing a naked sword with a nick in it as if he expects trouble. The nick isn't good. It will shatter in the next battle. I shake my head knowing there's nothing to replace it with.

"Under the promise of peace?" I press.

"For now," the man answers. He wears the red baldric of one of the king's captains. Before my father's death, I wouldn't have had the rank to be allowed to address him directly. "They rode in bold as brass, their leader bright as a sunbeam. Asked for the king, and the fellows nearly wet themselves bringing the lot of them here. Even their mounts are nervous-making. They weigh as much as a feather. They sparkle in the sun."

He shakes his head.

I tilt my head to the side in a question and he keeps talking.

"Their leader ... the King of Iceheim. He's with them. Their king." He looks around and then leans in close, clearly troubled, clearly needing to show it only to someone of equal rank. Someone he doesn't owe protection and confidence. "Why would they bring him right into our camp under a flag of truce? Maybe it's a ruse. Maybe it's a trap. But he *looked* like a king with that shining gold hair and his fair face, pretty as a maiden's. He claimed the banner of truce to treat with us."

I nod my thanks and put a reassuring hand on his shoulder. He's barely older than me – perhaps two and twenty – and my confident touch seems to calm him. I can offer nothing else but at least I can give that. Comradery in the face of turbulence.

I follow the boy.

This is why I've been called, then. If talks are possible, it will require all the king's knights and lords. I am one of them. Therefore, my presence is requested.

It's hardly necessary. I will give anything for even a temporary peace. I will serve under their yoke and be their beast of burden if it could save Castle Tor and the vassals left to me by my father. But if that were possible it would have been offered long before now.

Likely, they have come to demand our surrender and the heads of all our nobility. That's what they did when they rolled over Marvalan and took that kingdom. I'd give them my head if it truly bought peace. But I have spoken to women who fled Marvalan after their nobles gave their heads. What they endured after the collapse was no peace. The memories of their stories still keep me up in the cold hours of the night.

I'm still pondering that, still black of mood and energy, when we enter the tent and the boy scurries aside. The last to arrive, I take a quiet place behind the other knights and lords. We stand in a half-circle to one side behind the seat of our king. It's cold enough that my feet and fingers hurt, but no one shuffles or stamps to keep warm.

The king drinks something steaming and sets it on a low table where he plays merels opposite a golden-crowned fae holding a naked sword on his knees. It has too many gems. If they've balanced it for the gems, then the moment one is dislodged the sword will be ungainly. I wouldn't want a sword like that. Simple is better.

The fae king looks up from his game. If he's as good-looking as the vassal said, then I don't see it, but it's hard to tell with men. Even fae men. So, though I comprehend no loveliness in his face, what I see worries me enough. I see triumph. I see victory. I see disdain for us children of ash and dust.

And I'm surprised to see that behind him, in the other faces of the fae, there are glimmers of fear.

My eyes narrow. Fear? The arrogance I expected. The hints of contempt were almost a certainty. But fear? I am rarely surprised by what I see in the faces of men or fae. But I am startled now.

My king is speaking. He's the age my father would have been, had he lived. They were friends, I think, of a sort. He's young for forty, his hair still dark. The grim lines on his face not deep enough to age him.

"And so, you consulted this woman soothsayer, King Precatore of Iceheim?"

"I consulted one who knows her well," the golden king says with a sly smile. But the fae always look sly when they smile. It means nothing. He sprawls back in his camp chair, arms thrown wide, legs open and falling outward – at ease. Or so he would have us believe. "And I brought him to you so that you may hear his words from his own lips."

He moves his piece lightning fast. Why they play at all makes no sense to me. If it's to show their skill, well, they've been playing with men for two years. They've shown enough. Our land bleeds with their skill.

"And you claim it is a way to bring peace between our people," the king says, and I can't bite back my gasp. It's hidden by all the other sounds of surprise around me. Spines stiffen. Fists whiten.

Peace.

We can barely hear the word in this time, no less speak it. We want it with a lust more powerful than any other.

"If you want accord," my king says, "just stop the attacks. Stop them today and we all go home in peace."

"It's not so simple." King Precatore seems to take up even more space in his seat – to loom even though he's closer to the floor than all of us. He's a grand being – majestic and dominant. A king among kings. Something I keep tight inside wants to bow. I'd rather chew through my own leg than allow that.

"Tell me why," my king's voice is like a whip. His hand twitches like he longs to scrub his beard with it but is holding back. I've seen his daughter do the same.

Princess Cela is alike to her father in every way and just as disdainful of Castle Tor and its whelps as any other court lady – or rather she was. I've not seen her since she was fourteen summers and shipped off as bride to the King of Calernon in that ill-considered treaty that dragged us into this war in the first place. I watch the king carefully for any hint of her other tell, a one-shoul-dered shrug she used to give when she was losing and bluffing.

"I will not tell you why," this Precatore says coldly, though still, he smiles. This time, he lifts the goblet set before him and swirls it, filling the tent with the smell of mulled wine. My mouth waters. How long has it been since I tasted wine? "But I will let you hear the prophecy, and you can decide. Tell him, VIvar," he said, motioning to a fae behind him who is his opposite in every way.

Where Precatore is golden and decorative, muscled like a statue of a god, his armor gilt on the edges and gleaming, this man is dark, shadowed, and dressed plainly. He shrugs irritably and iridescent wings flicker behind his back. It bothers me that they can fly. Bothers me enough that I hate the winged ones the most.

"Who is this?" my king asks, moving his piece with care.

"My uncle's bastard. VIvar," the Iceheim king says, setting his piece down with a loud *click* on the word bastard. "Useful still, though not necessary. I have heirs from my first wife and backups from the second."

"Your adulation, as always, warms my heart, Precatore," the bastard prince of the fae says. He makes my mouth dry and not just because of the advantage those wings give. This fae is dangerous. "But let us not tarry. I'm eager to be rid of this place. It stinks of mortal blood and ambition."

"My favorite things," Precatore says, eyes guarded, as he sips his wine.

And there's the shrug my king has been trying to hide. He's worried. We're losing. If I was a cursing man, I'd be cursing now.

"Listen then, mortals and Court of Iceheim," this VIvar says precisely, like a scribe doing a burdensome duty to a strict measure. "If you want peace, listen to the words of the seer."

He closes his eyes to quote the words as if being careful not to get a single one wrong.

"The Golden Prince a bride must take,
A mortal crowned for amity's sake.
She who nearly usurped the place,
Of her with greater royal grace.
Thus bloodshed ends in solemn vow,
We kneel as one in common bow."

He sweeps one disgusted look over us and then says, "My duty is done."

King Precatore waves an indolent hand, and his half-cousin is striding through the tent, forcing a way through the gathered souls within, and gone out the flap before Precatore's taken another sip of mulled wine. For a moment, before the tent flap falls shut, I see the dark fae leap into the sky on those mayfly wings and I grip my sword pommel tightly.

"I'm sure even your mortal minds can understand who the Golden Prince is. Or do you need that part deciphered?" Precatore raises a mocking brow.

"You'll wed one of us?" my king seems shocked. I know I am. The fae do not marry mortals. They see us as disposable.

"Indeed, I shall," Precatore says. "For I want this curse broken, too."

"Curse?" I hear the word being whispered on our side of the ring and I'm as confused as anyone. What curse does he mean? We know of none.

Precatore stands, flourishing his cape. I realize with a start that he's won the game of merels while we weren't looking.

"Know this," he says with a sneer. "My armies will not stop fighting yours until my bride is brought, the vows are spoken, the curse lifted, and my people freed. Not for a moment. Not for a breath. If you want peace, bring me a bride and bring her here quickly."

He strides out of the tent, his people following him, and I catch the edges of horns and hooves and tails as fear and fury bubble in me. I bind them down yet again, forcing them from my mind.

We are all too stunned to say a word. Lips are parted, tongues licking dry lips, hands twitching for the hilts of weapons, and I see that desperate look in every gaze I meet. That look that is like seeing a man whose very bones are aflame.

The king stares blankly at his merels board where white has dominated. The rest of us whisper the words in everyone's mind.

What curse?

3

HALDUR OAKENSEN

"Can we trust this prophecy?" Lord Beecher asks after a long moment. We all look at him and he sighs. "What if we find a girl who fits this description? We tear her from the arms of her family and deliver her to the fae. Then what happens? The war just ends? Can we trust this fae king to do as he says?"

The question hangs in the air, snuffing out hope where it had flickered just moments before.

"What choice do we have?" my king asks. "They came to us on our lands. They would only have war from the very beginning. They claim some kind of curse is upon us all. Do any of you know of a curse? Have your people defiled tombs? Have you scorned otherworldly beings?"

We look at him helplessly. If anyone has done those things, they are long dead. There's not a glimmer of understanding in any eye I meet, just confusion and fear.

He sighs.

"If we do not try to offer them the bride they request, then we watch the remainder of our people whittled down until there are none left but the oldest and the youngest. We are almost there already. Will we send children to face these monsters? Will we surrender and leave those under our protection to face what other kingdoms have seen done at the hands of the fae?"

"Who would give a daughter to them, though?" Lord Beecher asks with a shiver.

Around me, feet shuffle and gazes turn down. No one wants to offer a daughter.

"My child is already sold for peace," the king says heavily. But I expect he's relieved. She's married to a human man. Whether she chose him or not, it's a better fate than this.

"It's not a matter of volunteers," Sir Weaven says eventually. He's young. Not even twenty and five. He has no daughters or sisters. For him, this is merely a puzzle to be solved. "It's a matter of finding this girl. *She who nearly usurped the place, Of her with greater royal grace.* Who is that? Was there some noble girl who nearly usurped your daughter? Was there ever a question of that?"

The king is shaking his head, but he looks troubled.

"Can we trust the bastard?" another voice asks. Sir Gherhin. One of the few still in his prime. "The half-cousin the king presented to us? There was no love lost there."

"Bastard," Old Huldric mutters. But he isn't cursing. He's thoughtful. His old lips tremble when he speaks, purple and blotchy in the cold. One of his eyes is milk-white and blind as a moonless night. "Usurping. Hmm."

"You have a thought, old friend?" my king asks, his

eyes burning with intensity. If we have only one chance of peace, he will root it out and force it to fit.

I understand.

I will do the same.

"Your ..." Huldric begins and then pauses. He's the lord of Castle Fairfield and a favorite of the king. They raise his hunting dogs there – or did. I don't know if they still do. No one has ridden in a hunt for animals in a very long time. What we hunt now are magical shadows, half man, half beast, all demon.

The king waves impatiently over whatever awkwardness has made Huldric pause. "I will take no offense at any suggestions."

"Your liaison with my niece is well known though not spoken of," Huldric says quietly and the king's cheeks – to my surprise – flare scarlet. "Her daughter was born a single day after your legitimate heir. And by our laws the oldest inherits, legitimate or not. She was but a day shy of usurping her place – though perhaps you do not know. We did not speak openly of it."

"Where is she now?" my king asks, and I snap my mouth closed on censure.

He does not know. He has a daughter who ought to be in his care, and he does not know her day of birth nor her whereabouts.

I grip my sword pommel tighter. I must not show the others how aghast I am at this willful irresponsibility. Honor demands loyalty. That my king will publicly admit a lack of honor makes something I hold tight crumble.

I discard it. Anything that crumbles cannot be kept. I

have not the strength to bear broken things along with everything else. I have my vassals to defend and lead. I must occupy myself with that.

The conversation has gone on without my attention.

"Sir Oakensen," my king says, and my head snaps up. "You'll ride, then, with any of your men who can find good mounts. Make all haste to Castle Fairfield and retrieve my daughter and the Lady Fliad, granddaughter of Huldric. That should serve propriety."

There are murmurs of agreement and some grimaces as they look at me. I do not look like a reputable escort for a king's daughter, even an illegitimate one. They send a known lady with her as a guard for her reputation.

"Lord Huldric's people will provide mounts for the ladies," the king continues, but my mind is a blur of organizing and planning.

Can I bring them all? How many horses can I find and from where? How fast can we ride out? The men are tired from battle – but we must ride for the last hours of daylight.

At least I can tell Fergan that the chances of getting hot food will increase the further from the army we go. If I can bring Fergan. I will have to leave him with any vassals I leave behind. Hard to find horses these days. Even poor ones. I'll ask the picket master.

My mind is so full of orders and demands that I hardly notice being drawn almost bodily from the command tent. Hardly notice as Old Huldric leans in to whisper in my ear in his trembling way, "She's a good girl. Mind her well. And take the boy with you."

If she's a good girl, why do none of them seem to

realize that they plan to offer her up to a monster? I look at him from the corner of my eye as a horse might do when it no longer trusts the rider.

The messenger boy is thrust toward me. The one who needs feeding.

I want to object that we will be in danger. That we will ride hard. That there is no place for a child. But I take one look at him and melt. Perhaps, I will find him a meal, too. Perhaps, he can even stay at Castle Fairfield when we get there. The name conjures images of horses grazing and sheep scattered over green fields. It's winter, but that doesn't seem to matter to my imagination. I cannot leave him in this hellish mess after imagining him there.

The boy looks up at me hopefully and I nod to him.

"Promise me you'll look after him," Lord Huldric says, and I meet his eyes and realize this is what he cares about. Not curses or riddles or even this war, just this one scrap of a child.

And in that glance, I realize he's thinner than he should be, shakier than men his age are, even in these advanced years. He might not live to see me return. Has he been giving the boy his rations?

"Say it," he begs, and his hand reaching for me shakes so hard that I grip it just to steady him.

"I so vow," I agree.

And then we slip away, me and the boy, and it's finding horses – too few – and packing bedrolls and water and breaking the news to Fergan that I've only found a dozen mounts and he'll have to stay here to lead the vassals I must leave behind, and it's me giving him my second-best blue tabard so he can carry my authority, and then me bidding farewell those we cannot take with us – too many – and then we're off.

We make an odd party, a knight who is not a knight, a dozen tired vassals, an eager scrap of a boy, and a happy dog.

4

IVA FITZROY

"**I**va!" The voice startles me Especially a panicked voice like this in a place of sanctuary. It has the sound of a sheep fallen down the well or a barn on fire.

I'm careful to place the warm puppy beside his mother before looking up. She starts licking him immediately, though she's not finished birthing her litter. It's warm and dark here but if Gretsha doesn't stop shouting it might trouble Fern too much and we'll lose a pup in her anxiety.

I turn slowly so as not to startle Fern. This is her first litter and she's doing well despite the worried look in her sharp eyes. She's a high-strung dog – perfect for hunting – but not perfect for whelping pups. She needs to borrow my steadiness, my confidence, my strength. I keep my hand on her shoulder when I turn and place a finger to my lips so that Gretsha won't speak loudly again.

She scurries into the stall with me, her braids almost

dragging in the warm straw as she scoots to the side to avoid the warm brazier full of embers that I've set to keep the stall warm. Her eyes are bright with excitement and tension. At nearly eleven summers, the whole world is still full of possibility for her.

"Soldiers rode in," she whispers in my ear, reaching into one of the reed baskets I've woven and bringing out a patch-blanket to pull around herself. I've made it plain that any castle children who visit my kennels are welcome to cuddle in the straw just like the puppies. "A dozen of them and a boy. Lady Fliad and Lady Stepha are speaking with their commander. You're bid to come and join them."

"Me?" I'm surprised by that. I work in the stables. I sleep in the back with the ostlers and dog handlers of which I am one. Most of my time is spent with the dogs – breeding and training them for the king's hunts, but I work just as often with the horses. Maybe that's it. Maybe they need their horses tended and the usual groom who meets visitors is not available. "Is Brona not here then?"

"Brona has the horses," Gretsha says. "Don't you hear her settling them?"

Now that I'm paying attention, I do hear low voices and hooves on boards, nickering, and snorting. The sounds of horses. But there are always horses here and quiet, well-trained dogs. No one is baying or barking.

I fix Gretsha's braids and pull a strand of nettle-vine out of one of them before offering her a scone from my pocket. She's been busy hauling water. I can tell by how she shivers. It's work too hard for a girl her size, but I was busy with the whelping when I should have been assisting her.

"They all have weapons," she whispers. "They look like they're here to fight. They look like the wild dogs that linger on the edges of the fields when the sheep are birthing."

Maybe they are here for hunting dogs, then. I look worriedly at Fern. She's in no condition to be sent to the king and neither is Ash with his cough nor Willow with her torn paw. That leaves just three others – good breeding stock and well trained, but only three. The king hasn't wanted dogs in years, and we've allowed breeding less and less to keep the numbers down. Dogs are expensive to feed. I have to ride with them on the hunt at least once a week just to keep our meat stores high enough to sustain them.

I nod and whisper, "Did Lady Fliad have a task for you?"

Fliad can be harsh, but she's forgetful enough that the younger vassals get off lightly. Even when we were girls and she enjoyed ordering me about she would grow bored easily and I could escape. But now that her mother is ill, her father dead and her grandfather at the war front, she has the managing of Castle Fairfield.

Gretsha shakes her head and I pat her gently on the shoulder.

"Stay here," I whisper. "Watch Fern. Don't touch her or the puppies unless you have to, but someone has to make sure that none of them touch the hot brazier, and if Fern is having trouble you need to call for help. Can you do that?"

She nods happily, already settling into the straw. She'll probably nap and that's fine, too. We get little enough sleep with all the menfolk gone. The castle still needs keeping even if there are half the hands to do it.

I slide a shawl around my shoulders and hurry out of the barn and into the courtyard, wary at first. There, in the center of it, spaced around the well and taking turns drinking from the dipper, are a dozen men and one boy. They hang back as their leader speaks to Lady Fliad, his helm tucked under one arm respectfully. His eyes are cast down in a mild way. Gretsha was wrong. They aren't here to fight.

I wait for a break in Fliad's words to suggest feeding them. The soldiers are as grey as their clothes under those worn blue coats, half-frozen out here where ice frosts every post and knoll.

"This letter is in my grandfather's hand," Lady Fliad says sharply to their leader. She's dressed in some of her finest clothing, her hair caught up in a delicate net and the thick outer robes she wears are trimmed in white rabbit.

Her mother, the lady Stepha stands at her right shoulder, wavering with the effort of standing outside. We will be lucky if she sees the spring. The cough is deep in her lungs, and she is losing the battle to it.

Fairfield's last living counselor stands at Lady Fliad's left. Somehow, he managed to find a chain of office, though the soldiers can't have been here for long. His rheumy eyes sweep over them sightlessly. He's too old for his place, but there is none other to take it up.

Fliad flicks a hand at the open letter as if she has

forgotten he cannot read it. "Its contents make no sense. You're certain it was put into your hand by Lord Huldric?"

"Mmm," the man she speaks to says.

He's wearing a tabard with a blue eagle stitched on the breast. That makes him a knight, though he's young for one. Twenty summers, perhaps. A bare summer more than I. At his side is a dog. I'd guess the dog to be perhaps six years. Not a hunting dog. A mutt. But she watches me with clever eyes and her lines are sleek and fast. He's been feeding her. Maybe more than he feeds himself.

The knight hasn't noticed me, so I study him carefully. He's thin – too thin – like all his men. Just as hollow-cheeked but with their same stringy muscle as if that's all that's left of him – a set of bones and some rope keeping them moving. His looks are plain: his nose too large, his hair cut very short for war, rather than allowed to flow over his shoulders. His short beard is dirty, just like his clothes and the backs of his hands. How long have they been traveling? They look as though you could push them over with a finger, and once they toppled, they'll fall into an enchanted sleep.

My fingers itch to mend their tears and feed them cook's soup. They need to sit a spell and be tended.

I clear my throat, keeping my voice deferential. Fliad doesn't like raised voices. She's been known to dock pay for a tone that's too high or too loud. Not that we're paid more than food and shelter these days. Docking that would be devastating.

"Would you like me to take the men away to eat, my lady?"

At the word *eat*, their eyes get too bright. It almost hurts to look at them – especially the child. I offer them a welcoming smile, letting my gaze drift over their hunched forms. Every hand is on a weapon, and I don't think they even realize it.

It almost hurts when I catch the gaze of the knight. There's a terrible sadness behind those eyes and an emptiness like a granary at the end of winter.

His hand flexes and the dog under it whines slightly. To my surprise, she leaps and before I can blink, she has her face buried in my hands. I can't help my smile at her silky fur and gentle nuzzling. She must smell puppy on me. Must know what that means.

I look up, wondering if anyone is upset, and for just a moment, I meet the sad knight's eyes. For the barest gasp – long enough for my heart to beat once – he flickers a smile. It's gone the next moment, but it was present. I saw it there. There is something about how fleeting it is that makes me think it's more precious than stamped gold coins.

"Away?" Lady Fliad says, and I don't know why she looks at me with fury. Her jaw trembles the way it did when her father died. Have we received news of tragedy? Her grandfather, perhaps? I swallow. Fliad – sometimes I still think of her as my childhood playmate – presses her lips firmly together before speaking again. "I hardly think so. Come here."

I come to her side, keeping my eyes demurely down. The dog follows me, nudging my fingers until I stroke her head. I do not look up until Lady Fliad sniffs.

"It seems your lineage has come calling, Cousin Iva. You're leaving your kennels and stables for good."

At that, my gaze finally whips up and I hope she can't see how my heart feels like it's sinking. I'm to be turned out. Where could I possibly go when every village, every croft, is just as desolate as this place? Only the nobility needs someone good with horses and dogs and those are my trades. Weaving baskets and sewing clothes are not enough to commend me. In the past, perhaps I could have married. There's no one of marriageable age in the whole kingdom except those fighting on the front. There will be no luck from that direction.

Fliad smirks at me as if she has read my thoughts.

"My grandfather writes me to tell me that you are to be married. And I am to accompany you to the front to see it done."

"Married?" I say and I don't recognize my own voice. "To whom?"

"To a king," Fliad says sourly. "Though why they choose my aunt's illegitimate progeny," she shoots a look at the knight with those words – if he didn't know about my shameful roots, he does now – and then returns her raven's gaze to me, "when there are ladies of blood to be had, I don't know."

She smiles tightly and her mother puts a consoling hand on her arm.

"We must make the best of it," Lady Stepha says before coughing a long, aching bloody cough.

"Yes, Mother," Lady Fliad agrees, and there's a flicker of pain in her eyes. If she goes to the front, she will not see her mother again. We all know that.

"I ... I ..." I say feeling as if I've been knocked from the back of a horse at speed. "I'm not of noble blood."

"Even diluted, king's blood is worth something in these matters," Lady Stepha says between coughs. She is never kind nor cruel, simply there being noble.

Fliad does not look like her, though I do. My mother must have been similar in face and form for we two are of the same brown skin, the same huge eyes, and waif-thin forms, though mine is hardened by work and scarred with marks of a life working with my hands while hers is so delicate a strong wind could blow her away. The rabbit fur of her collar makes her look like prey.

"Which king?" I ask. For what else is there to say. My fate is sealed, noble or not. The warmth of the kennel and stable exchanged for the coldness of a stranger's bed.

Lady Fliad and her mother look away, and Lady Stepha's cheeks flush hot but neither of them will answer me.

After a long moment, someone coughs and it's the first time I hear the knight's voice.

"Precatore of Iceheim," he says, and it sounds like a curse.

5

HALDUR OAKENSEN

We ate.

We had bought food along the way here and had our first hot meal in weeks on the road but sitting in the kitchen – for the lady of the house did not invite us to her hall – and smelling the freshly baked bread as it came from the ovens and thick hot stew in the kettle over the fire was not like eating on the road. It is a kind of heaven all on its own.

I am not above closing my eyes and savoring every bite, the same as my vassals.

"Do you remember cook's cranberry buns? At home?" Horace asks me in a whisper.

He almost looks his sixteen summers again. I offer a brief smile to honor that. It hurts to see him so happy – to see them all sated for once.

We're given rooms in a drafty, unlived-in space in the castle. With the men all gone for years and years, the hearths are cold, and the hasty dusting is not enough to clean everything. We do not care. Most of the men are asleep the moment they roll their blankets across the beds. I do not set a watch. There is no need here and everyone should be allowed this one luxury – a night of peaceful sleep.

I wash from a bucket hastily. None of my clothing is clean, and there's no chance to clean it unless I want to stay up all night. I, too, want the luxury of sleep. But I have responsibilities yet.

I must speak to the castle matron who takes the place usually filled by a steward. I wonder if Castle Tor has appointed a matron. I couldn't even guess who they might choose. This one is a strong-bodied woman with a hard face. I like her immediately.

She nods approvingly when I explain what gear the two ladies will require and what limits we must place on weight and size. They must ride horseback with some haste, but it is winter, and we must keep them from freezing.

"You'll take good care of our Iva?" she asks when I'm finished explaining. I'm surprised by her question, and it must show because she adds, "Of both of them?"

I nod my silent agreement.

"She's the heart of this place, sweet Iva," the matron says. "It will be a cold winter without her here and who will tend the pups?"

"Pups?" I ask and that gets a small, knowing smile from her as if she realizes how rare my voice is.

"She was helping Fern whelp a litter when you arrived but it's her first litter and dogs can lose a few the first time if they aren't helped. They're the king's dogs, you know. His hunting dogs, though they're raised here."

I nod. Perhaps that's where Hessa has gone off to.

"They need care," the matron says. "And I have none to spare for it with Iva leaving."

I swallow to prepare to speak. As always, I think hard on what I want to say before I open my mouth.

"There's a boy with us," I say.

She nods. And, of course, she knows because she will have assigned him a space to sleep.

"He needs to be fed," I say, not sure how to say what I need to say but she's still nodding, so I twist my jerkin in my hands and force the rest out. "He could stay in her place if you have someone to guide him."

The boy isn't mine to take or leave. But if I can do this much for him – give him a home in a castle, at least for a little while – then I'll take whatever consequences are dealt out.

"Why are you taking our Iva?" the matron asks, and I wish she'd said yes or no instead. I don't like things hanging in the air waiting to be finished.

"To end a war," I reply eventually, and I startle when I feel her old hand on my arm.

"I'll take care of your boy, Sir Knight," she says. "And you'll look after my girl."

I can't meet her eyes. I can't nod. But she seems to take my agreement as granted. It feels like an escape when I leave her to go find the boy – Jarl – and Hessa.

They're both in the kennels. I find them after searching the stables and getting hot snuffling greetings from the horses. I turn a corner to where the dogs each have an open stall. Their heads lift when I walk by, but they make no fuss about it. They're pretty dogs, all sleek lines and beauty. It does the heart good to see them.

I turn a corner and find the boy and my dog in a warm stall filled with clean straw. There's a sleeping mother dog with four puppies curled against her belly on one side of the stall, and a glowing brazier full of hot embers on the other. In between, Jarl is fast asleep, his young body curled against Hessa. She looks up and lolls a tongue at me, but her head is in the lap of the girl I'm going to deliver to a monster.

I think I smile at them, but I don't know. I feel torn up inside like a man gutted on the battlefield. I'm happy for Jarl. I can see his future – for at least the next few months – and it's full of nights like this. Good nights in the warmth with a full belly. But the girl smiling at me now will pay for it.

She motions me to sit, and I start to shake my head no, but I can't finish it when I see the pleading in her eyes, so I sit on the straw opposite her, so tired I want nothing more than to curl up in the straw like Jarl and fall asleep. The heat of the brazier warms me right through, but I must not relax completely. There are too many things I hold in tight that must not come unwound.

"He's happy here," Iva whispers.

Her smile gives her face a friendly warmth. I can't stop watching it. I've barely seen a woman these past few years. I've certainly not seen one close to my age, except for the Lady Fliad this afternoon, and she was not like this. She was cold and hard and beautiful in the way the ice is over the river. This woman is soft and warm, and her big eyes are full of kindness. I have not seen much kindness. This much of it hurts to be near. I want to shy away from it.

I try to form words and have to try again.

"He will stay with your dogs," I say eventually, and her smile widens. I didn't think it could do that. It hurts worse than the time I took that spearhead to the thigh. Hurts just like that wound where it burns for a moment and then aches afterward.

"That's good," she says, shifting her hand to rest on the boy's head for a moment before returning to Hessa. My mother used to do that when I was a boy. My throat feels tight.

I nod insensibly. I can't remember what we were talking about.

"It's a strange thing to put everything I own into a small bag and ride away. I've lived here my whole life, you know," she says, and I don't have anything to say in reply, but I don't want her to stop. Her voice washes me like warm water on a soft fleece.

I try a nod. It seems to work.

"I made everything you see here," she says with a pensive smile. "The baskets along that wall. The blanket. The wooden cups and dishes. I like working with my hands." She colors a little as if that were a confession. I've heard confessions that kept me up all night after the confessor was long dead. She shouldn't blush at this. "I cannot take it with me."

It's not right that she can't. Don't brides usually arrive with dowries? Things from their homes? I don't clearly recall, but there was some fuss about how to fill the ships when the princess was married.

"But I will miss the dogs most," she says, and I would have known that without her telling me by how she looks at them. She rubs Hessa behind the ears. "Is this dog yours?"

I nod, swallowing as I prepare to speak, but she carries on.

"Have you seen this king I will marry?"

I nod.

"And you were there when my father declared it must be so?"

I nod again. It doesn't feel like enough.

"I cannot defy the king's wishes. Particularly not during war," she says but she looks away and her face is unhappy. "Tell me about him?"

"Your father?"

She laughs quietly. "I suppose I could ask that, but I doubt I will need to know him. Tell me what you saw when you met the man to whom I'll be given."

"I saw..." I pause, thinking about how to deliver the blow. When you strike, it's best to be merciful. Kill quickly, inflicting as little pain as you can. But I find I do not know how to do this with words as I do it with a blade. "A fae king. Glorious and bright. Powerful. He wore too much gold."

She bites her lip and I know I am not doing this well. "And his temperament?"

"Arrogant. Confident," I say and yes, I'm certain I've done poorly.

Her hand shakes. I've wounded rather than killed. A slow death.

I wince.

"Has he anything good to recommend him?" she asks eventually.

I pause and think.

"In marrying him you will forge peace," I say at last. And that is the only good that I can offer.

Abruptly, I find I cannot contain my misery. Perhaps it is the warmth that has let it slip.

I lurch to my feet and hurry away without a word of goodbye. It's churlish and yet I cannot help myself. I was close, for a moment, to slipping. I'm hovering along that cliff's edge where tears and despair lie and I learned long ago not to walk that edge, much less fall into it.

I find the cold bed assigned to me, roll myself in a blanket, and embrace the small death of sleep.

6

IVA FITZROY

We ride at a breath-taking pace, driving the poor horses hard. Lady Fliad had demanded the best of the stable for both of us and I flinch when I think of how hard we are pushing them. Wildsage – Lady Fliad's horse is a grey mare, and her milky mane and tail are meant for careful brushing, not for clumps of ice and snow. Her eyes roll whenever we stop to rest the horses, walking beside them instead of riding. I don't know if it's fear that has her dancing so nervously or the way Lady Fliad saws the reins to keep her balance. I need to get that horse away from her, or at least warn her about what she's doing before she ruins the mare's mouth beyond hope.

My own mount is not the usual unflappable Tipper – my favorite of the castle mares, but rather Flicker, her foal, now grown to a high-strung gelding. He's Lady Stepha's horse and no more fit for this journey than Wildsage. I soothe him with gentle words and calm hands and try to give him his head as much as I can. He feels more certain when he has more control. Perhaps, by the time we reach the front, he'll be calm enough to take a less generous rider.

We've only been riding half a day when we reach the furthest point out from the castle that I've ever been – the small village of Courtey. I've been there only once before. It passes by so quickly, I scarce have time to notice anything new. The people scatter at our fast trot down the road leading through the village, a chicken squawks irritably, and then we're gone and easing into a canter.

We ride in a pattern, walk, trot, canter, gallop, get down and walk beside, and then through the sequence again with most of the time spent walking, or walking beside the horse, and short bursts of faster riding. It's the fastest we can move without spare horses, and we have none of those.

My goodbyes this morning were as chilly as I suspect my welcome to Castle Fairfield had been. No one wanted the king's cast-off then, and no one was sad to see her gone now. No one in the big house, at least. The other vassals will miss me, and I will miss them. I will miss the sense of home I had among my folk, working hard for the castle. I'd expected to spend my whole life like that.

Perhaps, in another time, I might have married another vassal and moved to a cottage just outside the castle, but men are thin on the ground now. Most women my age will never marry. To say I am surprised to discover that I have a different fate. That is a surprise. I hadn't thought that my father's unwillingly-given blood would determine much of my future. I'd been badly mistaken. What else might I be mistaken about?

I find I like the cold breeze in my face and the steady rhythm of riding and stopping. I can lose myself in the motion. I can lose myself in the goal.

Occasionally, my thoughts drift to the boy I left in charge of my dogs. Occasionally, my eyes drift down to the dog running alongside the black stallion at the head of the soldiers. Sir Oakensen runs side by side with her when he dismounts his horse, and her doggy delight is clear. She might have spent a single night with me in the kennels, but she is his dog through and through.

My one regret is that I could take no dog of my own with me. I asked Lady Fliad before we left if I might bring Whipper and she snapped at me.

"You aren't owed a dowry, Iva, and you won't be getting one."

"Not as a dowry," I'd said meekly. "But we have some dogs who are ready to live out their days before a fire. They'll miss me sorely. Perhaps I could bring just one with me? The loss would not remove anything from the castle's wealth, and it would soothe both my spirit and his."

"Marrying a king should be salve enough," she said bitterly, as if she thought that I did not yet realize how much she wished to marry the fae king herself. "You'll take no dogs from us."

Perhaps she wouldn't be so frosty if she had seen the melancholy knight when he described my future husband. I had to clench my jaw very tightly last night to keep a tear of self-pity from forming when he told me I'd marry a golden, arrogant man. But I didn't dare shed a tear when I looked at him and his vassals. Their worn clothing and weapons, their lined faces and haunted eyes, spoke of men who had fought this war to the very bone. Who was I to say I would not fight, too? Who was I to say that they should bleed for our country, but I would not?

So, I'd said nothing, and I'd been able to hold back tears even once he'd left, channeling all my feelings into preparing the dogs for my departure.

We pause now at a small bridge, and the soldiers are quick. One lights a fire, another jams sausages onto sticks to roast them – I recognize cook's handiwork there – while a third chops into the ice on the stream. There's nowhere to sit, so we stand ringing the fire, warming our hands, cooking the sausages, and eating them while they are still hot and bursting with juice.

"Trail is up ahead maybe an hour," the scout calls as he rides up to us, dismounting quickly to bring his horse to water with the others. "Only our tracks on it from the ride in yesterday. We can camp in the same spot."

"Mmm," Sir Oakensen says.

I wait to see if he'll say more, but he only leans into his dog and offers her a third of his meal. She eats quickly and then presses her forehead to his and lifts a paw. She's somehow more eloquent than any of us.

"You don't mean for us to sleep out of doors?" Lady Fliad says, horror in her voice.

The knight gazes at her steadily as if he is rehearsing what he plans to say before he says it. When he speaks, his tone is mild. "We will have many days of hard riding to your grandfather."

"There's no need to leave the main roads," Lady Fliad insists. "There are inns along them and good smooth roads. Proper feed for the horses. Proper food for us. We can't live in … this … for a week."

She huddles into herself closer, looking around her at the cold that forms white pillars from our breath and the steam rising from the snow where the sun hits it.

We wait for him to reply, but he says nothing. Eventually, one of his men speak – Rangen, I think.

"Begging your pardon, lady," Rangen says with a quick glance at Oakensen as if for permission. "The roads don't run straight to where we're going. It would double our time."

"Then we double it," she says, looking at Sir Oakensen.

He doesn't meet her eyes.

"We double it, don't we?" she insists, her voice growing high in pitch. "You wouldn't ask a lady to sleep in the snow. Exposed. I'll die. And for what? To deliver this girl to the army a breath sooner? It's not worth it."

He speaks then.

"Peace," he says and the soldiers around him seem to melt at the word, as if he's made the sun rise with it. "Peace must not tarry."

There is a weight to his words, like a judgment.

I walk carefully to Lady Fliad's elbow and ask quietly, "Can I help you with your horse, my lady?"

She's shaking her head, clearly furious, and so upset she can't find the words, but she lets me guide her gently away.

"What's wrong with my horse?" she demands the moment we're free of the men's ears.

"I think his mouth is hurt."

It is as good as time as any to check and see and it draws her away from what might be a powerful conflict.

She calms as we examine her horse. The mare's mouth is swollen and painful.

"We can swap horses," I say. "While I tend to her."

She nods, but she's not looking at me. Her gaze is inward, thinking and brooding and I can only hope she finds some kind of equanimity for I have none to lend her. I'm stretched and strained with the looming future, and I'd cede to her the role in a heartbeat if I thought I could.

7

HALDUR OAKENSEN

I finish scouting and return to camp to find everyone settling in. The firewood we hid under a pine tree the last time we were here is still dry and the men have our low, close tents erected, water boiling in a kettle on the fire, and food prepared. The fire tosses an orange glow and black dancing shadows everywhere, as if it is trying to make up for our lack of merriness all on its own.

I check over Hessa, making sure her paws are in good order. She patiently allows it before demanding her due in affection. Together, we walk the picket line, checking the horses. Hessa watches the trees and the forest around us with the attention of a dog who is hoping for a meal of squirrel.

The horses are in good shape for the most part. Rhurc's horse has a stiff foreleg. I run my hands down it but can't find an injury. Hopefully, a night of rest helps. Horace's has a small saddle sore. I'll have to address that with him. The grey mare that Lady Fliad was riding –

and then Iva after her – shies when I try to inspect her mouth. It's hurt. I frown and think back to the journey, remembering how the lady stumbled along when we were afoot, holding onto her horse's reins.

I'm pushing her too hard. Ladies aren't meant to travel so, but every day that we delay is a day that more men die.

The thought of peace still makes my hands shake. It feels like a dream that cannot last past morning waking. If it could really exist, then it must be brought in time to save as many lives as it can. Even if it comes at a terrible price. I think of Iva's big wide eyes and the cold golden king with the pointed ears, and I don't realize that I have my forehead pressed against Hessa's or that my breath is sawing in my lungs until a throat clears behind me and I turn to see Rhurc.

I release Hessa, drawing in an embarrassed breath and she whines, batting at me with a paw.

"I've set watches, as you ordered, and we're checking over the weapons and supplies. Rangen tore his coat, but the Lady Iva is stitching it for him. She's a dab hand with a needle. Doesn't seem right to see ladies sleep in a tent."

I give him a long look. Where would he have them sleep then? Out in the wind? They'd be much colder. I stand, and Hessa takes a place at my heel.

Rhurc clears his throat again. "The Lady Fliad has retired to the tent. We saved food for you."

"Thank you," I say, and I follow him. I'm not sure why he's so jumpy.

I find out when I get to the fire.

Lady Iva is stitching – and not just Rangen's coat, but

a whole heap of things that have been laid beside her. As I fill a wooden bowl and begin to eat, I watch her.

"If you find me willow tomorrow, I can mend the basket, too," she says to Rangen as she ties a knot and bites it off. "See if this will do."

She helps Rangen into his coat and smooths it over his shoulders and I see him grin like I haven't seen in months.

I glance around the fire and his expression is echoed all around. There are smiles and light in eyes that have been like empty hearths for a long time. I see evidence of other stitching and small repairs. She's been busy.

A sudden pang runs through me, and I bring my palm to my heart to still it. It's a memory of home – the home I once had. The smell of roasting meat. The sound of voices singing. The embrace of my mother. It makes my eyes and mouth water, and I have to fight hard to shake it, to force it back down into that place next to my spine where I keep all the things that might ruin me. This is no less dangerous than the fear I hide there. No less dangerous than the despair. It may be worse, because hope is infectious and brittle. You can catch it on the wind, only to see it shatter in your hands like a dry stick.

Hessa trots to Iva and lays a doggy head on her knee to claim caresses.

I can't bear to watch more.

I won't be required to guard until the third watch. I eat my food quickly and tromp through the cold to the tent I share with four others, roll into blankets thrown over the sailcloth that in turn sits on a bed of snow, and shiver myself into place. Maybe Rhurc is right. Maybe this is too hard on ladies to sleep in this frigid mess but the need to hurry is worse now, for my men have been infected. If I fail to give them peace now, if I don't give them that taste of home, what will become of them?

I think of that, of each of them returning to the warm arms of living loved ones, to lives of honest work without monsters or slaughter, to warm hearths, and someone with big eyes stitching their clothing and laying tender hands on them. And I wonder if they'll realize after it happens – if it happens – who we all sold to get it. I wonder if I'll ever feel peace knowing I helped deliver her up as the price.

8

IVA FITZROY

"I can't get warm," Lady Fliad says the next day, and I don't blame her.

I can't get warm either. I slept only fitfully between shivering and trying to get comfortable enough to sleep, finally succumbing for an hour or two when Hessa crept into our tent and spread out beside me. Lady Fliad was not willing to lie so close, not even for warmth's sake.

"We're made of stuff that shouldn't mix or even get too close," she'd said with a sniff when I'd laid my bedroll beside hers. As if we didn't already share blood ties.

I want to take offense. I want to say I can't help my illegitimate birth and I try to be useful, but if I'm honest, I don't deny that she's suffering right now for no benefit to herself. If, for some reason, I were to slip and foul the rules nobles have for themselves, her reputation might be ruined. Just riding to the front, even with me as companion, might be enough to do that. And then her hopes of marrying well will be gone forever and that's what noble girls do. They marry well and are happy to do it, or they do not marry and are miserable. It's not like she could take up work in the stables and kennels like I can.

So, I try not to take offense. She's only protecting the one thing she has – possible marriage to someone like Sir Oakensen over there, not that he realizes that. He hasn't so much as looked at her even when she's arranged herself prettily on her horse with her skirt fanned out artistically, or when she sat next to him to eat the porridge the soldiers cooked for morning.

"Can we purchase warmer things in the next town?" she asked him. "It's terribly cold at night. I need ten times the blankets."

She'd simpered then, trying to catch his eye on her pretty blushing cheeks and burnished hair, but he seemed to be looking through her before finally saying in that tight way he has, "We must make haste. The horses will slow if their burden is too great."

Judging by his vassals' expressions, that was a long speech for him.

"But surely just a few more can't hurt," she'd pressed.

He shook his head.

Lady Fliad's eyes narrowed at that, her breath gusting in the cold. "You carry food for that dog, and I've seen you ride her up on the front of your horse when she's tired. If you can have an extra luxury, why can't I who is above you in birth and rank?"

He'd stood so suddenly, that I had worried he might knock over the porridge pot. I'd made a grab for it, pulling it to safety, to the annoyance of Hessa who had been lounging with her head on my lap.

He hadn't even spoken, just stalked away, leaving Lady Fliad gaping until one of the men asked if she was going to eat her porridge and if not, could they have it.

We're far down the road and it's nearly noon when she finally shakes herself and looks at me. We've stopped for a moment beside the road. The soldiers heard something – though what they are worried about so far behind the front, I don't know. They've broken into three groups to scout for what it might be. One group has ridden ahead, and one behind.

"I can hear a creek running through the woods over there, Iva," Lady Fliad whispers to me. The guards stationed with us are spread out, staring intently down the road in either direction as if certain we'll see an attack. "I'm so thirsty and my waterskin is empty. Could you just step into the woods and fetch me a little water?"

I look nervously around. Everyone is spaced so far apart that none of them hears her.

"Please," Lady Fliad pleads. Flicker dances nervously under her. He needs the calm of a confident rider. "I'm so cold. I'm so thirsty. Is it too much to ask my vassal for a drink of water?"

It was a reasonable request, except that our guards were on full alert, and they must have a reason for that.

"I don't think I should go without the soldiers' permission," I reply, biting my lip. I'm defying her by saying no. She could have me flogged.

"Need I remind you that I am your lady?" she presses with a cold expression.

I feel a stab of fear through my heart. She doesn't

need to remind me. I know full well. I take the waterskin from her hands and start to dismount.

"Take the horse with you. It's foolish to walk," she commands.

The mare rolls her eyes as I urge her toward the deep snow off the path. She's still not recovered from yesterday and I don't like pushing her even enough to walk to the creek. She moves, but she's not happy.

The moment we're in the tree line, I can't see or hear anyone. I bite my lip and press on. I can hear the creek, which is strange since we had to cut a hole through the last one. It feels like it's close, but the more we press on, the more it feels like we are no closer. I pause after a moment, torn. If I keep going, I might go too far and delay our party. If I turn around and go back without the water, Lady Fliad will be furious. And still thirsty.

Anxious, I press on. It's snowing now – thick and sudden, like dropping an armful of down over your head.

Here it is – the water, at last. It's not a creek though, but a raging river, still open at the center with thick bands of bubbled, uneven ice on either side. I tie the mare to a slender birch tree and then creep across the ice on my belly and carefully refill the water skin.

My hands are painful and red when I'm done, but I have the water. So far, so good.

I stumble back to the mare, cold to the core now, and untie her reins with fumbling fingers. She snorts at me, and I can't even see her clouds of breath through all the snow. It's in my eyes and coating my hair before I can get my hood up, soaking my cloak and chilling me right through before I even have the knot free.

I've only just loosened it when the mare rolls her eyes again, sets her ears back, and nickers. I try to grab the rein, but it slips away, and she leaps, bounding like a snowshoe hare and leaving me alone beside the noisy river with her tracks already fading in the snow.

9

HALDUR OAKENSEN

I hadn't planned to stop in the town. It's only midday when I reach it with the scouting party, and I would have liked to get another half a day's ride closer to the front. There's a shortcut from this tiny hamlet that cuts straight through the heart of the forest, just like the little-known path we took to get here. It means more rough sleeping, but that's a small price to pay when men are dying and we hold in our hands the key to peace.

I've only just reached the town when the snow starts to fall – thick and full. I lose sight of the inn almost immediately, whistling so that Hessa won't lose her way – not that dogs do, but I worry about her.

With a sigh, I whistle and my men gather in close. In moments, I have them divided – two to speak to the innkeeper. We'll stay in the inn or the stables, whichever will have us. I have a few meager silver that the king gave me for expenses. Probably not enough, but I will make it work by any means that I must. I press my lips together in an unhappy line at that thought. I don't want to cheat the innkeeper and yet I have vassals who depend on me, two women, and just as many horses.

I sigh as I send a rider to bring in the groups behind us.

To my surprise, Lady Fliad's escort – the main group I left guarding her and Iva – enters almost immediately on our heels. I flick an urgent glance at Gragor when his face becomes clear through the snow. He slaps palm to heart in salute and draws in close.

"Barely made the town. Wind's so bad I couldn't see the path. Good thing the lady insisted on riding hard on your heels. Said she had a bad feeling."

My mouth goes dry as I count those riding past.

"Where is Lady Iva?" I ask.

"Isn't she with you?" Gragor pales as he asks the question. "Lady Fliad said she was riding on ahead."

I give him a level look. Gragor doesn't lie. It's not in his nature.

"We'll stay at the inn. Make haste," I tell him, but I'm already moving to intercept Lady Fliad.

She's riding with her hood pulled high and I don't get her attention until we're almost at the inn, a well-kept building with a clean front and shoveled paths. It does the heart good to see a sturdy building and diligent workers, but I've no time to relish in the wholesome effort.

"Lady," I call to Lady Fliad, leaping off my horse to catch up as she dismounts and hands her reigns to Rhurc. Beside me, Hessa yips uncomfortably. "Lady Fliad."

She turns to me with a placid smile. "Sir Knight. Will we sleep in an inn after all?"

I duck my head in confirmation, an abbreviated nod, and then force my question out. "Where is the king's daughter."

"Is she not with you?" she looks so innocent that I wonder if I'm leaping at shadows. "No, perhaps she was with the rear group. We were separated."

I nod, turning to go. I'll look in the last group. Someone would have noticed if she tried to wander off. Just because I feel ill at ease with Fliad, doesn't mean she's done anything that warrants distrust.

To my surprise, Hessa is licking her fingers. Fliad turns her placid smile to me again.

"If we are staying here, may I bring the dog in with me? She seems to want to warm up, too."

Hessa looks at me with huge, hopeful doggy eyes. She probably smells something tasty inside.

I wave a hand permissively and they're already opening the door to the bright lamp-lit inn and bringing in a flurry of sparkling snow with them before I've finished mounting.

After these years, you'd expect me to be more suspicious, but I wasn't. I just let them go while I rode back to the rearguard with certainty that the king's daughter would be with the last group.

They straggle in one by one, red-nosed, eyelashes and hair thick with snow. Rangen is the last by my count. The last except for Iva.

"The girl?" I ask him but he only looks at me with confusion.

I shake my head, biting my lip.

"Something untoward, Sir Oakensen?" he asks me, trying to look in every direction at once. "Were there signs of the enemy?"

I shake my head. "The girl is missing."

His face goes ashen.

"We didn't see the main group after we split from them. By the time we rode back to where we'd left them, there were hardly even tracks. You'd be hard-pressed to find anyone in this."

I grunt, turning my horse. Hard-pressed or not, we must find her. She holds peace in her small rough hands.

A whiny sounds, and then a white body emerges from the snow. A white body running full tilt, mouth lathered and eyes rolling. I spin my horse and race to catch up, snatching up a rein flapping in the wind, and riding with the mare through the snow until she slows. Rangen is there a moment later, his own mount puffing. I hold the mare's rein out to him.

"Go back to the inn and report to the others that I'm riding out to look for Iva. See to this horse. Protect the Lady Fliad. Make sure everyone is fed and rested," I order grimly and before he can object, I kick my horse into a trot toward the whirling fury of the storm.

Snow thick as frosting on a Turnsyear day treat. No horse. No experience living rough. If I don't find Iva tonight, she won't be here tomorrow.

I would like to say that as I ride into the mind-mazing storm, I have peace on my mind. That I ride for the sake of us all, but what I ride for is the girl who sews torn coats and sits in the straw with fresh born puppies and doesn't complain even once about the cold. I ride for a person. And I wonder if that will make a difference when the time comes to offer her up.

10

IVA FITZROY

She couldn't have forgotten me. I know that much. Although, it's possible that by the time she decided it was worth worrying about me, the snow was already too thick for anyone to find my tracks. Between the sound of the river and the blowing wind, I can't hear anything else. They could be within easy sight if it were a sunny day, and I wouldn't know they were searching for me.

The wind whips my cloak away from me, tangling it out behind me no matter how closely I clutch it to my breast and chilling me right through. I use one hand to keep my hood up, trying to keep it from my aching ears and smarting cheeks, but my fingers are cold despite my leather gloves, and they're losing dexterity with every moment.

It would be easy to blame Lady Fliad for my predicament but it's my own fault. I knew better than to go off on my own. I knew I should have turned around when it was farther than I expected. I should have known that

Wildsage would spook with her sore mouth and these strange surroundings.

I follow what I think is my own trail, bent down as much with regret as I am by the elements.

What are you supposed to do in a storm like this? Make a shelter? That seems so obvious when you say it, but I look around and there's nothing suitable for that. Whoever it is that wanders around prepared for any eventuality could probably do that, but I have what I'm wearing, a freezing cold waterskin, and my belt knife. While it's pretty stout, I don't think it's going to make a shelter all on its own.

I suppose I could hunker down under a tree and freeze to death slightly more slowly in a slightly less discoverable way. It has no appeal to me.

This feels like such a silly way to die – on my own, an afterthought as always, forgotten on my way to marry a king who only wants me for a chance sliver of royalty in my bloodline.

Put one foot in front of the other, Iva.

I shake my head – or maybe I'm just plain shaking. The cold is really getting to me. I'll never be warm again. I wish I could be home in the kennel with the dogs and the brazier.

Or even just the dogs.

Put one foot in front of the other.

I wish I could be cuddled up to Hessa and all her warmth.

One foot in front of the other.

With that deliciously serious Sir Oakensen curled up against my back.

One foot.

Yes. That would be nice.

"Lady Iva."

Yes, that's what his voice sounds like. All burred and aching like he's the saint of tears crying on behalf of mothers everywhere for their lost children.

"Iva."

I run into something solid. I look up, and if there's any warmth left in me to blush, then it's blushing hard. I was just thinking of him nestled up against me. I was just thinking of kissing his very solemn lips. They are frowning now as he looks down at me.

He takes my hand and I startle. He waits patiently, ignoring the swirling snow that stings my cheeks and makes my eyes squint against the icy blast. His cheeks and ears are bright red, too, so he feels it. He just lets it savage him without stopping it.

He leads me by the hand, silently, to his horse, which stands a little aside from us, obediently waiting. The stallion must be well trained. He bows his head against the wind but is otherwise as unflinching as his rider.

"It's a long ride to safety," Sir Oakensen says to me, his jaw tightening and then loosening again as he tries to help me onto the horse.

My legs and hands don't want to work properly. I fall twice, the second time sliding hard against him and we're both left panting and gasping in the lee of the stallion's warm back. There's concern skittering through the young knight's eyes. He licks his lips, opens them to speak. Pauses.

"By rights, I should build a shelter and a fire and warm you before we ride to the village."

There's a village?

His face is inches from mine, leaning in close so that I can hear him over the wind. I can feel the warmth radiating from his skin and count the snowflakes on his eyelashes. I'm surprised by how thick they are – dark like his short-cropped hair. He shaved his face at Castle Fairfield, but the beard is already growing back.

"Once," he pauses like this is hard to say. "Once we were caught out like this in a storm. Malchor fell through the ice. We warmed ourselves in a shelter under a tree. No fire. There were enemies about. We had to press our skin to one another for warmth."

Now I'm the one swallowing. Was I not just thinking of him cuddled against me? Only he'd been clothed then. I blink back sudden visions of him a little less clothed. I'm on my way to be married to someone else – at least if I don't die here. Dreaming about the knight charged to deliver me there is not my right.

His halting words – when they come – are like cold snow on the face.

"In this moment, that would be more foolish than dying of cold."

I feel my lips fall open in surprise at the harshness of his words. He's a kind person. I've seen him with Hessa and his men. I've watched his gentle tolerance of Lady Fliad. He's not harsh. But his words still sting.

"We must have peace. You understand?"

I think this is saying a lot for him.

"I don't think I d – do," I say between numb lips.

"Your marriage will buy us peace. The fae king has said so. The moment after your vows are spoken he will withdraw his soldiers and the dying will end."

Something burns hot and desperate behind those thick lashes and it's not desire for me or any woman. It's desire for peace. Longing for an end to war. I feel like it's infecting me, catching alight my own heart.

I nod and he nods with me, and I realize our faces are so close that my hair has fallen into his face.

"You need this," I say but it's too bare, too personal. It feels like an invasion, so I soften it with, "We all need this."

And his nodding now is fervent.

"There must not be the barest hint of impropriety," he says firmly.

I nod my agreement and this time when he draws back and tries to boost me onto the stallion, I struggle until I'm on his high back, clinging to the wet hair that smells of horse.

Sir Oakensen mounts the stallion behind me and turns him into the swirling snow – snow that looks the same on every side to me, but somehow, we are on a path that he can make out. He guides the horse through the fury of the storm – and through our wet layers upon layers of clothing, I can still feel his warmth at my back and that and the memory of his burning eyes keep me clinging to the back of the horse until we walk through the parting snow and are suddenly inside a small hamlet, stopping beside a snow-encrusted inn, and trying to bend frozen limbs to dismount.

11

HALDUR OAKENSEN

I nearly didn't find her in that storm. How she ended up there without her horse and apart from the rest of us – well, I have my suspicions, but I do not know for certain.

I scrub my hand over my face with relief as we ride. It also helps to clear the thoughts that have been cycling around and around in my mind. Thoughts of warming her by a fire. Thoughts of warming her with my skin. Thoughts I have no right to entertain. I'm honor-bound to protect her and lead her –unhurt, yes, but also untouched – to her bridegroom. I am not he. More than that, if I look at that with open eyes, I will admit – even to myself – that in a choice between marrying this girl myself or using her to buy peace, I would still buy peace. The thought of that sets my teeth on edge. I'm proud of my resolve and disgusted with my heartlessness all at once.

I try to turn my thoughts to the mystery of her disappearance. Should I question her? Should I investigate it?

We're days still from our destination. I must not allow this to happen again. But stirring up matters with Lady Fliad can help nothing. And if it was not her doing, then blustering at Iva for her carelessness will also not prevent future danger. She's cold through and miserable. That's enough warning for anyone. My men do not need lectures. They will already be hanging their heads at their lapse.

I'll let it rest but redouble my own efforts. That's the solution.

We reach the village in a cloud of snow and just in time. My stallion is huffing and worn. He needs stabling and a good rub down.

I dismount and help Iva down as Rhurc comes running out to take my reins. He won't meet my eye and a flare of worry shoots through me.

Horace, Rangen, Gragor, and Trellan come pouring out the inn door. Gragor's eyes are red. They should all be abed by now. My worry ratchets up. I look around us. Is there an enemy threat? I see nothing in the swirling snow.

"We were seeing to the horses," Horace says and Rangen makes an annoyed sound in the back of his throat like he thinks this is a poor beginning but too late to start again now. "None of us were there. We didn't see it."

"See what?" I ask but I feel ice forming in my belly. I don't like the sound of this. I gently steer Iva into the direction of Rhurc and I hear him murmuring to her about going inside the stables to warm up while he settles my stallion. Good. She'll be safe with him.

"He had a pair of snowcat kits," Gragor says, looking miserably at the ground. "The Lady Fliad bid me look at them, and as I was leaning over them, he grabbed me by the neck and hauled me back."

"Who?" I ask.

"A knight from Castle Rainsdale. Returning from managing a problem on his lands," Rangen says, and his face is pale. "We convinced him to wait for your arrival before he carries out ... well, he's calling it justice. We told him only you can determine a sentence for your vassal."

My belly rolls and my throat tightens. I look from face to face. The four of them have the look of men who are about to be ill and Rhurc has vanished with Iva like a child fleeing the wrath of a parent.

"He blames me for their deaths," Gragor says heavily. "But they were dead already when I looked at them. I touched them and they were cold."

I grunt, thinking fast. "There were witnesses."

"The Lady Fliad," Rangen agrees, but he doesn't look relieved, and Gragor puts his head in his hands. We're all coated in snow now and none of us cares. "But her testimony is damning."

I glare at him until he says more.

"She claims he killed them. Out of spite. For an insult to your person as a knight."

"What insult?" I ask.

"The other knight made a coarse joke about you searching in the snow for Lady Iva. Lady Fliad claims that Gragor killed the snow kittens as retribution."

I let the air gust from my lungs. I'm exhausted. I'm

cold through. My belly is a gnawing hole within. I feel unequal to the task of unraveling this.

Two nobles – the knight and the lady – with testimony against one vassal. Fourteen-year-old Gragor. If they demand him whipped and I don't agree, then I will have to fight the knight. That, I would do. But the lady is another matter. She will bring it up with her grandfather. If she does that, then anyone present here will have to pay the honor price. Which could be our lives. Not just mine, but all my vassals.

"He wants you flogged?" I ask Gragor and to my surprise, the boy breaks.

I've seen him in battle. I've seen him freezing by the fire. I've seen him starving. I have not seen him sob like this. I look away, aghast. I don't want his back marred, but I did not think to see him take the suggestion so hard.

Rangen clears his throat. "He wants his head. Tonight."

My gaze snaps to his and we share a heartbeat of understanding.

It's Gragor or all of us.

Everyone knows it.

Something hot and red burns through my thoughts even as I try to form them. I grasp at them but all I find are the ashes of panic.

Deep breaths.

Take deep breaths.

I slow myself down. I grasp my helpless rage and draw it into that hidden place next to my spine.

"Where is he?" I ask.

Rangen tips his head. He'll lead the way.

"Gragor," I say, and his head snaps up. "Help Rhurc with my horse."

He scurries away as if running to the stable can let him flee this. Best to keep him out of whatever comes next. I wish I could run, too.

I enter the inn forcefully. I must present myself as a firm wall or my vassals will suffer for my weakness.

The common room is just a small room with tables and stools and a long bar on one side with a door set in the wall behind it – likely to the kitchens. I see a face I don't know peering from the shadows of the door. The innkeeper, probably. He doesn't want trouble.

There are stairs just past the bar to the rooms above. I don't know if my men bought any rooms or if we sleep in the barn tonight, but no one lingers on the open stairs. The common room is empty except for Lady Fliad, who has a hand on Hessa's head, and a man I do not know.

My eyes flicker first to Hessa. She's smiling at me in her doggy way. Not hurt and not in danger. Something loosens in my chest. She sits back on her haunches and whines, but Lady Fliad doesn't remove her hand and Hessa won't move until she does. That's just dog manners.

I swallow and turn to the man. He's perhaps twenty and five, a full hand taller than me, and well-muscled. Still, I'd fight him for Gragor were it not for Lady Fliad. The death of a knight, I might cover up, though it would haunt me. The death of a lady would be impossible to disguise.

She watches me with a penetrating gaze. He, with a

calculating one. Beside him, the corpses of his young cats are laid out on the table beside his supper. A curious way to treat anything to which you're attached.

"You call a claim on my vassal," I say without preamble.

"You must be Sir Oakensen," he says, spreading his hands in greeting and smiling widely. It's the smile of a man who has never known death or doesn't care. The latter is more dangerous, but the former can bite harder in ignorance than he would if he understood. "I am Sir Rainside the Younger, and yes, I have a claim on the life of your vassal Gregor. He has killed my brace of snowcats."

"You're not at the front," I say. I can smell tonight's dinner, but hungry though I am, it only turns my stomach.

"I had business," he says, leaning back in his chair and offering Lady Fliad a knowing glance. She shares the look with him. They've arranged this together, then. Why? I can't see it and that bothers me. "As did you, I hear. You're busy guarding those precious to the king."

I don't say anything to that. I won't be baited or played.

"And in the course of business, one of your vassals has harmed what is mine – a priceless pair of creatures are dead, their lives unredeemable. They would have grown to a breeding pair and now I'm out my investment in them as well as their lives. I demand a life for a life."

"You won't have it," I say grimly my eyes flick back to the kitchen door, and to my surprise, I see the innkeeper is not alone there, hiding in the shadows. Rhurc is there and so is Iva, tucked in tight beside him. My breath hitches in my throat.

"Then I will plead my cause to the king when we reach the front," Sir Rainside the Younger says easily. "The Lady Fliad is my witness, both to the original crime and now to your failure to uphold the law and exercise your duty as a knight. If we testify it will mean not just the boy's death but yours and all your vassals present tonight."

A dozen dead for one boy. And yet I will not give him up. I believe his story.

"Lady Fliad?" I ask, raising a single eyebrow. Will she truly testify to this lie?

"What would you have me say, Sir Oakensen?" Her eyes widen innocently, though I do not think her guiltless. "'Tis a grave deed. And to see you forsake your duty is just as troubling."

I clench my jaw against her words.

"I see, perhaps, another way," she says, idly playing with Hessa's ear as she speaks. My sweet dog settles down on the floor, wiggling slightly as if she longs to greet me but is being patient. I long to hold her, too. It would loosen something that is growing tighter around my heart.

"I long to hear it, fair lady," Sir Rainside says. I despise his honeyed tongue. "For I am not a man of violence and would be sore grieved to see it done."

Not just honey-tongued but fork-tongued. No word of that is truth.

"You have lost two creatures of great value to you," she says with a sweet smile and wide eyes. "A great tragedy. You ask for a life for a life, and that is fair. But why take a human boy when you could request from Sir Oakensen another creature. This pleasing dog which has been his, I hear, since boyhood."

I lurch a step forward before I stop myself, and I want to scream when I see the look of knowing pleasure in Sir Rainside's eyes before he widens them artificially and says, "Why lady, your proposal is as wonderful as any the Great Seer Mervelin could have devised. Truly your wisdom exceeds that of women."

I force myself to steady calm, but my hands are shaking, my grip tight – painfully tight – on the pommel of my sword. I can see in my mind how it could go. A quick draw and one fast step forward, arcing it over my head and around in a double-handed strike, and I could have his head off. Slight pivot and a backhand and hers would join it.

No.

I force myself to breathe. Unwrap my fingers from the pommel one at a time.

If I do that, we will all pay. And I will have taken two lives that are devious but not worthy of a death sentence.

My breath shudders through me.

"Hessa," I say, reaching for her, but Lady Fliad grips the skin of her neck so she can't come forward. My dog whines, more insulted than hurt, but the sound aches through me for I know what comes next.

"I don't think so," Lady Fliad says. "If you take her back first, who is to say you will relinquish her. She goes to Sir Rainside directly. Isn't that so, Sir Knight?"

"I am mollified, dear lady," he says with a sweeping bow. "The dog for the boy. It is agreed."

I haven't cried in five years. Not once. My vision is hazy now. I don't dare blink, or they'll splash down my face and I'll be unmanned before all.

I grunt, wheel, and I'm slamming the door open and striding into the whirling snow before I break and slaughter everyone.

12

IVA FITZROY

I sleep in a bundle of blankets in the stable with the soldiers. I offered to sleep in the second cot in Lady Fliad's room, but she laughed at me.

"Let's dispense with the fiction that we are traveling together to protect your virtue," she'd said. "We both know which of us is meant to sleep in inns and which in stables."

"Would you not like me to guard your reputation, my lady?" I'd asked and the furious look she'd leveled at me made my cheeks flare red and my mouth snap shut.

I am happier in the stalls anyway. There was only one room free in the inn and Lady Fliad is less warm than the drafty stall where I lay my blanket. Drafty it might be, but the warmth of animal bodies and the soft snuffles of the horses help me drift off in no time. The soldiers offer me the spot with the cleanest straw, kind even though they are skittish with fear. Gragor is bundled in a corner, his face hidden in a blanket and his shoulders shaking. I move toward him but Rangen stops him with a shake of his head.

I can't stop shaking, I'm chilled so badly from my adventure, but Rhurc silently brings me a mug of hot tea – a luxury! – and I drink it down as Trellan puts an extra blanket around my shoulders and rubs them through it briskly to warm me. They wouldn't treat a lady this way. Thank goodness I am no lady.

I don't wake until midway through the night when the door creaks. Nearby, someone moves in the straw. There's just enough light to make out the silhouette of a man with hunched shoulders and his head hanging low in despair.

Sir Oakensen.

He needs his sleep, but even now he turns and turns again in the straw, the relief of sleep evading him.

I saw Fliad take Hessa from him in that neat little trick. And now I know why she bid me leave her side and then rode off without me. She was planning this little cruelty. But why? Why trouble our guardian? Why distract him right when he should be alert? Why bid me sleep away from her room when all good sense warned us to stay together?

I drift off and wake to the faintest light of dawn coming through the crack at the bottom of the door.

"Wake them. We ride with the dawn," Sir Oakensen says to Rangen. His voice is even rougher than usual. I think he has been crying, though I don't think he'll ever admit it.

A candle is lit, and we rise, packing silently in the darkness. Everyone knows what happened. Gragor hangs his head with shame. I pat him on the shoulder.

"Not your fault," I whisper.

"Feels like it," he whispers back. He's blinking like he's holding back tears, too.

"Feelings don't always match the truth," I tell him gently. "None of your friends want you dead and that's what would have happened."

He looks up at that with a wry expression as if he isn't so sure of it himself.

"She was his only family left, you know. All the rest are dead. Just that dog. He's had her since she was a puppy. A last gift from his mother."

He chokes a little on a suppressed sob and I do the unthinkable and wrap my arms around him in a kind hug. It's not something a good noblewoman would ever do. But it's something I've done to comfort the goat boy or the cook's assistant when a goat was gored, or the biscuits burned. If we couldn't have the touch of another human to tell us we aren't alone when everything goes wrong, then are we human at all?

I go from one to the other of the men, offering help with bundling things on the backs of horses, with fitting bits into mouths and checking hooves over, with distributing hot tea and collecting wooden cups to wash after. I keep busy. I touch shoulders where I can and offer smiles. They drink in every touch, every word, every hint of a smile like parched ground, and I wonder if it's mothers they miss, or wives, or sweethearts, or grandmothers, and if they'll ever see them again.

Sir Oakensen said that they could have peace if I

bought it for them with this marriage. When they look up at me with those bright eyes, I want to buy it for them. But when I look away, I see only Lady Fliad's cold indifference and I wonder. If she – an inconsequential noblewoman, unmarried, unlanded – sees me as so small compared to her, what will a golden fae king think of me? Will I be of less value to him than a brace of snow kittens? Will he break my neck to force the hand of an enemy as I am certain she did to those cats?

I have no answer as we mount our horses, and she joins us in the stable yard with an arrogant sniff. I still don't know, as we ride out in miserable silence behind our mourning leader. The trail seems lonelier without a black dog on it. The number of our party seems reduced by half, the hope in their hearts, almost entirely depleted.

HALDUR OAKENSEN

It is day one of my life without Hessa. The world is a fog of red rage.

HALDUR OAKENSEN

D ay two without Hessa. We travel north toward the front. I think I eat and sleep. I am not certain. I know we cover miles. The men look thin and cold. The ladies harrowed. I cannot look at Lady Fliad without my hand drifting to my sword of its own account. I don't dare be near her, lest I succumb to my worst instincts.

15

IVA FITZROY

I can't sleep. Lady Fliad finally invited me to sleep in the tent with her again, but my mind is too full of gnawing anxiety and repulsion. The sight of her given over to sleep makes me feel ill. I know what she did. I can hardly bear to look at her. That disgust combines with anxiety. I keep seeing it all play out as I watch from the kitchen door. Fliad, gleeful, as she delivers a death blow. Her accomplice smiling maliciously. The knight I've come to rely on buckling as if from a blow. He's not the same now. It's as if he left his spirit with his dog and only the body rides with us now.

I slip from the tent, gathering my thick cloak around me. I sleep in all my clothing. It's too cold not to. The fire has burned down but the embers glow. I crouch down by its warmth, carefully laying a few sticks on the embers to wake it up. I could use the heat to chase the cold from my bones and my heart.

The camp is quiet around me, the soldiers all asleep in their tents except for whoever is on watch. I hear him moving around the perimeter of the camp, but it's so still that when I don't move, I can also hear the heavy breathing of sleep gusting in the tents.

I wish I had a cup of tea to calm my nerves. We ran out of the small store of leaves I brought yesterday. The men carry only the most basic food with them.

As the fire leaps into fresh flame, I draw my hands close and blink against the strong of sharp smoke. This moment, here, alone in front of the licking fire, might be the last free moment of my life. I'm not used to living so closely under the observation of others. I'm used to coming and going among the stables and kennels and in the fields, tied only to the rhythm of the daily chores and meals. Here, it is all watched and disciplined. When I am given in marriage to a stranger, I think it may very well be the same. I'll be an oddity in his world. A curiosity. Will I ever hold a sleeping puppy on my lap again or clean the hoof of a horse? Will I ever while away quiet hours in a field teaching dogs to come and go and follow? I think I will not. I think that I am losing what makes me Iva as surely as Sir Oakensen lost what makes him the brooding warrior these men follow.

He's there when I look up, and I'm not surprised. Whenever I think about him, he seems to be there. He crouches by the fire, and I pause to listen. No crunching of snow or scraping of twigs. He's the one who was guarding the perimeter.

"What's your name?" I ask him before I look up.

I see his feet shift position uncomfortably.

"Your given name," I specify, looking up now to meet his red-rimmed eyes. He frowns at me. "I don't know it, you see. You know I'm Iva Fitzroy. I know only that you are Sir Oakensen."

He nods, swallows. "Haldur."

His voice is rough. He's hardly spoken these past days.

"Are you still Haldur now that she's gone?" I ask him and our eyes meet.

He doesn't guard his gaze. It opens his soul for me like the opening of a thick oak door. All the light and darkness of what lies behind seems to pour out toward me.

I don't flinch from it. I meet it honestly with my own depths. And for this one moment, we share in something deeper than touch, deeper than the closest of intimacies. A moment where the quickening of one heart is matched exactly to the flow of the other, so that there is nothing separating the one from the other.

I see in his eyes the realization of it. I wet my dry lips and hold onto it for as long as I can.

"I don't know," he says, still looking deeply into my gaze as if he hopes to find the answer there. "But I will meet the demands of honor, still."

I could drown in just this moment. Breathe it instead of air forever.

"I don't think I will be Iva when I marry this fae king."

I didn't think his gaze could be any sadder, but it is, suddenly.

"But I will also do my duty," I say and my voice breaks on duty.

He nods, subtly. We hardly need nods or words just now.

He leans forward and I don't think he realizes he's

doing it. His lips part. And for a moment there's a flash of something deep in his gaze, something agonizing and beautiful all at once and then he drags in a shuddering breath, draws away and his eyes shut and close me out again.

He runs a hand over his face. There's a rip under the arm of his coat.

"I could sew that," I say, pointing to it. "It would only take a moment."

And so, I mend the tear in his clothing, still warm from his body as I hold it on my knees. The moment is gone, and yet it lingers like the warmth in this coat.

16

HALDUR OAKENSEN

Day three without Hessa.

I keep feeling the stitches where my coat is mended. I rub at them like a healing wound and my eyes drift to Iva where she works mending a harness as she rides her horse, or gently teasing Gragor until he can't help but smile, or stirring a pot beside the fire while Lady Fliad looks on with sharp eyes.

And if I weren't charged with delivering her to her wedding day, perhaps I could be Haldur again when I am with her. Her smile brings back memories of home. I can still smell her on my coat from where it brushed her long dark hair while she fixed the tear. She mends more than cloth. I see her mending my vassals as we journey.

She could mend me like that. She could stitch my tears back together. They'd still not be the same, but they'd be closer to whole, closer to salvaging.

I can see it all in my mind. Just like I can see what would have happened had I actually kissed her when I came so close to it by that fire. Just the memory makes my pulse pound in my throat and body throb with the memory. Only honor held me back from it.

But in my mind's eye, I feel her welcoming softness. In my imagination, I feel her gentle arms wrapping around me, drawing me into that warm place where all my tears and wounds are welcomed and I'm safe just to rest – even if it's only for a moment.

I swallow and wrap that dream up carefully in folds of wistfulness and tuck it down next to my spine where I keep all my burdens.

This burden is one I want to bear.

17

IVA FITZROY

Spring has decided to come with a joyous suddenness. I wake to the chatter of birds and the whole day is spent riding through snow that shrinks in on itself. The sun beats down with such heat that I let my hood fall and let the light wash over my face.

"Do you know what the fae lands are like?" I ask Rhurc who rides beside me.

"Shadows, is my guess," he says grimly, not realizing, I think, why I ask. "The fae look tangible enough when you aren't fighting them. They've faces like humans and those strange fox ears that end in points. Some have antlers, some hooves, some tails. There are even some with wings pretty as a dragonfly's or an eagle's. But the moment they attack you they change. They're shadows and fire then. Great raging, elongated things that tower and shift and fight with the strength and fury of the fires of hell. So, I would guess that the pretty exterior when they are at peace is a ruse and their true nature shows in the attack. I've thought on it a lot and I think their home must be shadows and fires, too."

"Nonsense," says Lady Fliad from behind us.

I startle at her words. She's hardly spoken since we left the inn. Hardly even complained. Her face is drawn and pale as if she has been worked to the bone, but she only rides through the day, just like us, though her hands twist constantly around a pair of gold amulets she wears around her neck on a chain. Even at night, she clings to it, whispering and withdrawn. Perhaps, she feels guilt over what she has done.

"The fae are little different from us except for their long lives, beauty, and magic. They live much as mortals do."

No one speaks to contradict her but after long moments Rangen says, "Well, there was some mention of a curse. Isn't that true, Sir Oakensen? There were rumors as we were packing to leave the camp."

Haldur has just ridden back from scouting forward. He takes that role more often than is required, I think. He looks between us now, as if puzzled by this conversation he's entered against his will. His stallion nudges Lady Fliad's mare – she's back on the mare now that the poor horse's mouth is healing – and he pulls the stallion away, making him dance a little at the force of the reaction.

"Isn't it true that the fae said something about a curse when they left the talks?" Rangen asks. "That's what was being said before we rode out."

Haldur grunts a reluctant acknowledgment. His eyes meet mine – just for a heartbeat, but they always do that now. Whenever he's within sight, he looks to me immediately before turning back to what he's doing. It sends a shock of heat through me every time. I'm so conscious of it that I think I could feel it even if it happened behind my back.

"Maybe the shadows and fire are part of the curse," Rangen says.

"Then why would they want that to end?" Rhurc asks. "Seems like an advantage to have over your enemy."

Rangen shrugs and Sir Oakensen clears his throat.

"Open stream ahead. We'll make camp nearby. Tell the men we'll take shifts to wash."

Sounds of approval fill the air. No one has been able to wash in days. Not even at the inn, with what happened there.

"Iva and I will take the last shift," Lady Fliad says imperiously. "Set our tent up so that we can dry within it, Iva."

Even she must be excited for the chance to get clean. She's calling me by name and asking for things rather than expecting them to simply be done. That's almost friendly by her standards.

I'm happy to be warm for once as I set up the tent and build up the fire.

"Can you start the soup?" Rangen asks me before his shift goes to the river.

Gragor is already back, wet as a fish and laughing for the first time since we left the village. Rhurc shoves him as they enter their tent. They look younger than usual. Almost as young as they actually are.

"Of course," I say with a smile, busily working to set

out food, mind the fire, bring fallen logs over for seats, and ready the wooden dishes. I use a pine bough to sweep the area around the fire to rid it of what snow and debris I can. Just because we're outside doesn't mean it can't feel homey. Will I be allowed to make a home when I go to the fae? Will I live in a house at all or will it be a cavern or a hollow tree?

I try not to feel a pang of fear at the thought of what life will be among another race – a race the soldiers claim is actually made of hellfire and shadow?

I bite my lip, and focus my thoughts elsewhere, missing Hessa. If she were here, I would have the comfort of her dog breath and dog grin. Without her, I'm the only one left to offer anyone comfort and I don't dare ask them to coddle me when no one is caring for them.

I'm just finishing the soup when the second shift of men returns from the river, shivering loudly, scrubbed red and clean, but smiling with the satisfaction that comes from clean skin and a fresh scent. Haldur is among them. He doesn't smile, but his frown lines aren't as deep and when his eyes search for me and find me he seems almost at peace.

I offer him a smile – a deep, calm one, the kind of smile I know he needs right now.

He rubs the back of his neck and looks away, and he, too, looks his age as his cheeks blush brightly and his wet hair gleams in the softening spring sun.

"Iva, attend," Lady Fliad calls, and I see her there with a length of linen and fresh dresses in her arms. She even has one for me – an act so shockingly generous that I am immediately suspicious.

I hurry to her side.

"The soldier there," Lady Fliad says, pointing to Rangen who bobs his head in acknowledgement, "says it is our turn to bathe. The men will give us privacy except for a single guard who will keep his back to us and stay on the bank."

She seems pleased with the arrangement. Maybe she's really getting used to this kind of travel. Her eyes are as bright as her shining gold amulet.

We make our way through a twisted path between the trees and then out of sight to where the river is open. Draping the dry clothing on the bushes, we leave Rangen there with his back turned stiffly to us. He's donned only his breeches and boots, letting the hot spring sun dry his skin. He almost looks like he could be going fishing with his weapons set aside like that.

Ignoring him, we strip quickly and leap into the water. The cold steals the breath from my lungs and for a moment, I'm flooded with memories of happy dogs hitting the pond water while the ice is still floating in chunks, their woofs filling the air.

We both hurry to wash, the icy water immediately reddening limbs and making everything tingle as if stabbed with pins all over. We're wearing one shift in hopes it can be cleaned with our bodies and there's a spare for each of us hanging with the dresses on the pine trees.

"You're still wearing your amulets," I warn Lady Fliad. She wouldn't want to lose them under the waves after all the time she has taken to keep them close. I blink. Seeing them clearly, they look almost identical.

Why wear two of the exact same amulet? Double the luck?

She shrugs, but though the movement is casual, there's something odd that shines in her eyes. I'm too cold to delve into it. I duck under the water to clean my face and hair, hoping to be finished quickly so I can get warm again. I rise from the water almost immediately, gasping in the cold like a caught salmon.

Something tangles over my head and around my neck and I'm still dashing water from my eyes before I see what it is. One of the amulets. Lady Fliad has put it around my neck.

Confused, I turn to her and gasp.

I'm looking at myself. That's me with those too-big eyes and wispy figure. That's my scar over the nose and cheek where a tree branch hit me when I chased Ash through a storm when he was just a puppy. That's me with the long dark hair and clinging wet shift. That's not me in those eyes, though. I don't think I've ever looked so calculating. She's wearing an identical amulet.

I gasp and look down at what is now an impressive chest and rounded hips. I hold out my pale-skinned hands – purple from cold. My golden hair, darkened by the river water, hangs in tangles around the gold amulet.

"You don't really want to marry the fae king," Fliad says with my voice. "And I do. So, this is a tidy trade. As long as we both don't take off the amulets, we two can both get what we want. I'm being reasonable. I'm making sure you benefit from this, too."

I'm seeing all those times she was pale and tired

clutching that amulet. How much energy does working magic cost?

I pause, not sure what to do. She's not wrong. I don't want to marry the fae king. With her body, I wouldn't have to.

There's a strangled sound coming from the woods, and my gaze snaps to it at the same moment that Lady Fliad's – my? – gaze does. Rangen lied. He's been peeking as we bathed and he's frozen now, on the edge of the water, mouth open in astonishment.

Lady Fliad moves like a hunting dog scenting prey. She's through the water and to the edge faster than I can get these unfamiliar legs moving. They're not very strong and I stumble in my first step, misjudging how much power I have to turn and leap. I lumber forward, but I'm too slow, too awkward in this body that isn't mine. Already, Lady Fliad has her hands around his throat and is dragging him under the water. She caught him off guard and by the way his eyes roll, I think he doesn't know if he's allowed to fight back.

She drags him under the water and bubbles roll up like a pot boiling.

And now I'm finally there, trying to pry her hands off his neck. I can't get a grip. Everything is too wet.

My thoughts are hot and racing, clumsy in their speed. I need to get him free before it's too late. He'll be down the river before anyone can stop it. I need to do it now.

My hands fumble, leaving gouges in her wrists, but she doesn't let her grip slacken at all. We're grunting and gasping, beyond words as she grips and I claw, and Ranger grasps my legs with weaker and weaker hands.

There's a splash right beside us and I don't have time to think of what it might be before I'm thrown through the air onto the snowy bank. I land hard, pain flaring through my hip. With a *smack* Lady Fliad lands beside me – still wearing my skin – and then Rangen lands beside her. Lady Fliad scrambles to stand and disappears, only to land again with a loud curse, but someone's pinning her in the snow, and I can't help how my eyes widen at the sight of *him* wet and dripping straddling someone who looks exactly like me.

I shake my head to clear it and scramble over the snow to Rangen. He's the one who needs me right now. I check his breathing. He's still alive but choking. I turn him to his side as he coughs out water, and then more water, and I'm too busy saving his life before he drowns on his own vomit to notice anything else until I hear the cursing.

18

HALDUR OAKENSEN

The soup I'm bringing for Rangen makes my mouth water as I balance it in my palms. I know our quick wash left me hungry as a bear in spring and he likely feels the same way. Best to feed him, or he won't be alert. I ease my way through the trees, looking for him. He's not on the path as I would expect, not even when I turn the corner and follow the narrow divot in the snow trampled just enough to make walking easy.

A strangled cry sounds from somewhere ahead and without thinking, I drop the soup and run. I don't have a weapon with me. It will be hand to hand. Still no sign of Rangen.

I break through the trees and onto the icy shore, my breath sawing in my lungs. Something distracts me, waving in the wind, and I sink into a ready position, but its only dresses hung on trees.

I pivot toward the water and to my horror, the two ladies are in the icy water fighting over something. Their medallions catch the light, blinding me, but it's clear that Iva is trying to keep something under the water while Fliad fights her off with all her strength. She's not very strong, being a noblewoman. Iva keeps her back easily.

They gasp and grunt, and it's all I hear along with their sawing breath.

I hardly know what to think. That they're fighting at all baffles me. Iva has never so much as protested anything Lady Fliad wants done.

A patch of wet hair emerges for only a moment is dunked back under and I gasp as I realize what they're fighting over. Rangen.

Betrayal makes me ill, but it doesn't slow me down. I crunch through the snow on the shore and launch myself – fully clothed – into the water. I don't know what I've done with the soup. Fury gives me the strength of three men as I scoop Fliad up first and fling her to shore, followed by the lighter Iva, and then Rangen – oh please don't let him be dead.

I'm trying to catch my breath as I emerge from the frigid current when Iva launches herself at me, her hands around my throat, throttling me, but she's a woman and her hands are small. I wrench them off and throw her to the bank again, leaping to straddle her and keep her down.

What madness is this? I feel like a man whose own sword has turned on him.

Fliad scrambles around us to get to Rangen and I want to stop her, but Iva claws my face, and I must settle her first. We fight and it tears my heart to pin her hands against the ice, to see them purple and bleeding, to see her soft flesh abraded and bruised under my hands.

I search for her eyes, for her warm eyes full of kindness, and all I see is a violent arrogance. I haven't seen an expression like that since the night Fliad stole my Hessa.

Wait.

My eyes flick to Fliad, tenderly nursing Rangen. He's coughing up water as she gently rubs his back and whispers to him.

Back to Iva.

"You've switched bodies," I say stupidly. That's why you shouldn't talk unless you have to. It comes out stupid.

Iva – no Fliad in Iva's body – lets fly a string of curses in Iva's soft voice and I'm so stunned I almost lose my grip on her. She shakes her head, snaps her jaw shut, takes a long breath, and then looks me directly in the eyes and I can't help it. Even knowing this isn't Iva, I can't help the jolt that goes through me when our eyes meet.

"I was going to kill the witnesses, but why kill you? Why not just ask you to agree?" she says and she sounds weary. "Why wouldn't you want this, too? I've seen how you are together. It must be eating you up to think of her with another man. But it doesn't have to be like that. I'm not married. No offers for my noble hand, but you're a knight and you could offer to marry me – her – and the two of you could live happily together. Don't tell me it's the body. My figure is twice what hers is."

I'm so stunned that I just speak.

"We need peace," I say grimly. "I'm sick to the point of death of war. My heart cannot stand more of it."

"I'll marry the fae king – this Precatore of Iceheim," the Iva that is Fliad says. "I care not if he's shadows and fire or antlers and tail. I was made for royalty. I was made for better things, and I plan to seize them if they are not offered to me."

I can see it all in my mind – fleeing all this. Starting a new life at Castle Tor with Iva. Me, working hard. Iva, mending my clothing and making soup and smiling that smile that breaks my heart with all its hope. It wouldn't matter which body she was in, I would want to be with her. I'd want to clutch her hand on dark nights and hide her in my shadow on dark days.

It's a tidy solution. Everyone would get what they want. But what if it didn't work? What if it was the soul that mattered and not the body?

"The prophecy is specific," I say between gritted teeth. I have a good memory and every word of the prophecy is ingrained within it. *"The Golden Prince a bride must take, A mortal crowned for amity's sake. She who nearly usurped the place, Of her with greater royal grace. Thus, bloodshed ends in solemn vow, We kneel as one in common bow."*

"Prophecies are only what people use to manipulate others," Fliad says coyly. And that looks she gives me fires my blood because my brain keeps insisting it's Iva looking at me like that. "And what I want is a throne. And what you want is each other." I feel my face flame at that. "What's so terrible about all of us getting what we want?"

I look at the Iva inside Fliad's body. Is she in on this? She looks away and toward the north, pain in every crease of her face. I do not think this was her idea but perhaps she needs to be reminded of that.

"By your honor, you must do this," I tell her simply. "By my honor, I must see it done."

And that's wistfulness in her eyes. I can see it plain as the snow under the sun. She wishes she could say yes. She's thinking about it, chewing her lip as she decides between freedom and the doom of marrying for everyone else's peace. I hate myself for what I say next. I hate that the words even come out of my mouth.

"If it's not you, there won't be peace. Would you give the lives of others to have peace for yourself? Would you give their futures for your own?"

I know she won't. I know what she's made of, even after such a short time, but it sickens me to hold her to this. I'm no better than the father selling her, or the king buying her. I bury my revulsion deep down next to my spine.

She looks like she might cry, but she shakes her head and rips her amulet off, flinging it into the river where the current will drag it away. I reach forward, not daring to wait for Fliad's goodwill, and I rip the chain from her neck, breaking the clasp, and fling it into the depths to join the other necklace.

Suddenly, I'm straddling the curvy Fliad and it is slight Iva trembling and miserable with Rangen's head on her lap. I can't help it when I scramble off the lady and lose the soup I just ate into the frigid river.

I couldn't save my dog. I couldn't save this girl.

Am I even a man at all?

19

IVA FITZROY

"They were given to me by a woman in a deep hooded cloak," Lady Fliad finally admits when I press her in our shared tent.

She's been crying. She can't stop shaking and I don't know if it's from the horror of what she almost did or the disappointment that she didn't succeed. I should put an arm around her. I should tell her everything will be well. I can't summon the words. I can't cross the tent to her side. I stand, instead, as far from her as I can, my arms crossed over my chest. Around us the canvas flaps and stretches against the bracing and ties, trying to yank itself free. But none of us can be free.

"It was the night before Sir Oakensen arrived," Fliad says, dully. "I scoffed when she told me I could exchange bodies with someone else. That all I had to do was hold the amulet tight and put my intentions into it for three full days and two full nights straight, and then put one medallion over my neck, and one over the neck of she with whom I wanted to exchange. I asked her why I would want that, and she brought down her hood just long enough for me to see her pointed ear, and then she told me, 'You'd make a lovely queen,' and she left."

I watch her in silence for a long time.

"Was it really so wrong?" she asks in a small voice. "It would have given all of us what we wanted. How could that be wrong? I still don't understand why you wouldn't agree."

I look toward the tent flap.

"Not all of us," I say, my chest constricting.

It's three days later that I slip from camp on my own, following my instincts down a small game trail. I can't admit what I'm doing, so I don't try. I let my thoughts freewheel instead.

I don't know what to make of Sir Haldur Oakensen. That he is a man of honor and duty, there is no question. That he would give my future for the peace of his people – again, no question.

But the searing looks he gives me whenever his eyes light on me, gut me. It's as if he opens a window to me that looks right into his soul, and it goes down, down, down into black nothingness – an endless pit of sorrow that cannot be stoppered.

Still, he looks for me whenever he goes and whenever he returns, only to offer up this aching present – a gift woven of pain and dashed desires. And I know he wishes it could be otherwise and the wishing is eating him alive.

I know, because I wish it, too. And I look for his glances. I meet his eyes on purpose, even knowing what will be in them. I want what I cannot have, and it is rot to my bones and pain through all my sinews.

"Two days' ride to the front," he says when I catch him alone, just as I knew I would. Just as I know I should not.

He stands in a patch of dry ground under a pine tree. The hot sun of spring has melted the snow around the tree and dried the fallen needles. I can smell them, dead though they are. They linger in the air, their scent an endless reminder of what is lost.

I move to stand beside him, kicking up more of the funereal scent.

Together, we look over the valley below. Far in the distance, I see a dark mass. The armies, I think. Watching them shakes something loose inside and I clamp my lips tightly together so its whimper will not escape.

He glances at me wildly, as if he can feel it, too. As if he is barely holding it back, too.

His lips part, and as we look into each other's eyes we share this helpless feeling together, this sad longing for what cannot be – for what neither of us thought was even possible before. Is it worse to know it could have been but is not, or would it have been worse never to know at all? I think I'd rather bear the wound of it forever than unbroken skin that knew not the knife.

He's shaking all over, and then to my utter surprise he bends slowly – oh so slowly, giving me all the time in the world to walk away – and he doesn't sweep me up in his arms. He doesn't press me so that our beating hearts are only separated by fabric and skin. He keeps his hands tight on the hilt of his sword as if it can defend him from this even as he succumbs. He stoops just enough to breathe my air and to softly – soft as a memory that flutters behind thought – press his lips to mine in a chaste kiss.

I think I weep at the touch.

My first kiss.

And likely the last touch by a mortal man. The last touch of skin from anyone who loves me, now that my dogs are far away, the matron of the house far away, my friends and fellow vassals behind me forever.

It is precious if only for its brevity, for the feeling of something stolen and given to me, something bought with a price too steep to pay.

And then he curses in a whisper, choking on the word so that it contorts on his lips, and he's gone, crunching through the last of the snow, leaving me there to breathe the scent of dead pine and look at my looming future.

20

HALDUR OAKENSEN

I am twice a fool. A fool to have given the last piece of myself away when I know I can never get it back. A fool to have acted on it for even a breath.

And I don't even care. I will give my vassals peace. And then I will ride away from here, as far as I can go, until no one knows my name or my sins. I clench my hands on my hilt and I try not to think about Hessa, and I try not to think about Iva being married to that golden demon, and I try hardest of all not to think of how I could have made different choices and kept them both if I'd just held my honor and the lives of other men more lightly.

We ride mostly in silence now, as we enter the valley. The joy of hot food and bathing in rivers has passed. There will be no more warm stables or guest rooms. There will be no more fresh food bought in villages. We are returning to the front, and even though we know that if things go well, it might mean we can return home in mere months, none of us can truly believe it.

The light in Rangen's eye has been dim since the incident at the river. He twitches whenever he catches sight of one of the women and his hacking cough keeps him hunched over his horse most of the time. If there was another village in which to stop, I would leave him there.

Rhurc and Gragor won't meet my eye and I can tell by how they shake when they look north, that their thoughts are haunted by visions of returning to the front. Of the fighting. Of the dying.

Lady Fliad has been silent. When she looks at me it is only with bitterness. I almost prefer that. She, at least, I owe nothing except the protection she has already received. Her resentment is easier to bear than the fear and misery that the rest of the band has been dipped in.

Iva is quiet, too. She still mothers my vassals, offering kind words and small services where she can. I find my eyes drifting to her when I am not willfully keeping them away. They turn to her as sure as flowers open to the sun. At least I have the strength not to speak to her, not to break and touch her without permission a second time, not to do worse and confess that she has carved a groove within me like the well-worn track of a cart that will never smooth over again. I will live the rest of my life hollow from her absence. If I can but keep that from her, then I will have finished my duty with honor. I have nothing else left to me.

We ride in silence but for the huffing of breath, the creak of leather tack, and the occasional *fump* of snow falling from the trees. Spring shrinks the depth of the snow hour by hour, bringing bits of sticks and bark to the surface as it disappears, revealing the hidden impurities.

That night our camp is soggy, and we dare not risk a fire. Raiders have been known to slip around the main army and pick off stragglers here. We are still off the main road, following game trails and trapper's routes. It's safer, but still not safe enough.

I go to sleep in a wet blanket with wet feet.

I wake to my last day.

And the first thing I do is look for her. She's huddled in a blanket and sitting on a log. Her eyes meet mine and she gives me a smile, as if she doesn't hold it against me that I kissed her. As if she holds no acrimony that I prevented her escape. As if there is still in her heart an undeserved warmth toward me.

I ought to say goodbye now, while I still can. But though I open my mouth, the words will not fall out. It is as if by saying them, I fear I will sever something beautiful.

Instead, I just stand there a long time and look at her while she looks at me. I don't want to stop. It's the only goodbye I can bear to give her.

And then Gragor circles in from morning watch and asks me a question and the moment is gone.

We ride through the morning, and I keep my eyes focused. There's a wind today, making branches squeak and howling through any open space. It makes it hard to hear so much as a report, much less an enemy, and the constant movement of the trees surrounding us keeps me jumping at shadows.

I'm peering into the trees on full alert and I still don't see them until they're upon us. I whip my sword out.

"To arms!" I'm still shouting over the wind when the first enemy leaps at me – a beautiful creature with long shining silver hair and the horns of a goat. He transforms as he leaps, his sinuous dragon-scale mail and narrow face consumed as he transforms into a creature of shadow and bright fire. I fight, spurring my stallion to stop and paw the air as I sweep my sword through where he was only a moment ago, pivoting to follow his whip-fast movements, my training and experience kicking in to make it a series of quick actions and reactions, precise, intent, and accurate.

It takes me too long to bring my enemy down. Too many movements, too many lunges from my horse. By the time I'm riding over him, I've lost track of those behind me.

I wheel to find them spread out, fighting for their lives.

Iva has a sword. She's brought it up awkwardly in front of her. Fliad is beside her and they're both on the ground. The white mare screaming and thrashing with a spear in her belly. There's no sign of the gelding.

A dark shadow dances before Iva. None of my men can get to her. Everyone in the circle around the ladies is engaged.

I plunge my stallion toward them, gripping my sword tightly and angling it for the charge. We strike as one, the horse and I. My sword slices the shadow monster through the chest. I manage to keep hold of the weapon as we wheel, but the monster is lunging toward the women now. I turn the stallion a second time but he slips on something – the mare, I think, with horror – and we go down hard. I keep hold of my sword, keep hold of my head, and find my feet beside him as he scrambles to find his. No time to check to see if he's uninjured.

I race forward instead, sliding into defense as Iva's first blow goes wide and she falls off balance, panting, beautiful, and far too vulnerable in her light dress and swirling skirts.

The shadow creature – the fae – gathers its body backward, preparing to aim a strike. I don't give it time to hit. Instead, I lunge forward – and it never stops surprising me that it works. Why do they give ground when I'm only man-sized and they tower higher than trees in these shadow forms? Why does my strike maim and kill when it seems to hit nothing but shadow?

No time to ponder. I dispatch the shadow with a series of quick strikes, jab, jab, slash.

He falls, the shadow fading and he's a she, it turns out – the most beautiful woman I've ever seen with hair like sunlight and a face that would break your heart were it not split in two with my last strike. Shame fills me, acidic as vomit. I have killed a woman, fae though she is. My ancestors will reel as they watch this stain me.

I do not linger. Instead, I spin, assessing again. Shaking off the feeling of nausea washing over me.

I count five heads other than the ladies. Only five.

My heart is racing, slamming against my ribs.

Only five.

There are more figures in the trees. They race toward us. I grab the reins of my stallion and call, "Gragor!"

He's still mounted. The only one who is.

I have the black in hand by the time he joins us, face white, red speckling hands and face. I don't so much as speak. I just grab Lady Fliad by the waist and fling her onto the stallion. She screeches – a fine way to thank me – and it sounds like as much outrage as fear. Good. Fear is infectious and the stallion doesn't need it.

Iva is next. I don't dare look in her eyes as I set her in front of Lady Fliad, shove the stallion's reins into her hands, and turn to Gragor.

"Ride hard and fast and deliver them to the king. We will cover you."

He doesn't need more orders. Neither do the women. And I've never wasted speech, so when I turn to them, I don't plan to say anything, but her eyes are like the moon to my tides, and they drag from me a single pained word.

"Go," I say, and the word rips my throat on the way out just like the goodbye in her eyes rips my heart from my chest. I may not live the hour out, but even if I do, it's unlikely I'll see her again.

I smack my stallion's flank and he leaps.

"Rally to me!" I call, drawing the others inward. "To me!"

There's no time for lingering gazes with Iva. I'm stealing short spears from the dead fae at my feet. She has a half dozen. We don't usually carry them but that doesn't mean I can't use them.

I already have one balanced on my palm in an over-head carry when a shadow bursts from the trees, lunging for Gragor. I toss the spear with all my might and a huff of breath. I see it strike true but I'm already pivoting for another, hefting it shoulder high and flinging it when the second shadow leaps for the ladies. He goes down silently. That's two.

There's a roar behind me and I drop the rest, lifting my sword just in time to block the blow crashing down on me and that is the last I see of anything but battle for quite some time.

21

IVA FITZROY

I didn't even get to say goodbye, I think stupidly as Fliad clings to me so tightly that I don't think I can breathe. We rode hard until the stallion began to stumble and then Gragor finally slowed us, letting us come down to a quick walk until we reached the road ahead.

"Not far now," he said then, but he was breathing hard, and I didn't think it was all from exertion. I'd looked him over but there were no wounds. I was still trying to puzzle out what was wrong with him when we met the first of the king's patrols on the road and he reported to them.

"Attacked an hour's ride south," I heard him say. "I was ordered to bring the ladies to the king."

"Your knight?" the soldier had inquired.

"Lost, I fear," he said in a choked voice, and that was when I realized why he was breathing so hard. It wasn't pain. It was grief.

It struck me like a hammer between the eyes, leaving

me so stunned that I hardly noticed as we were handed from group of soldiers to group of soldiers and hurried toward the front. Gragor knew war. If he said that Sir Oakensen – that Haldur – was lost, then he must know.

I heard names but remembered none of them, heard Lady Fliad ask questions and did not register them, saw the army thicken until we were surrounded by men in arms with grimy faces and dull eyes and I just kept thinking the same foolish thing.

I didn't even get to say goodbye.

I meet the king – my father – a man I have never laid eyes on before. I hardly care. He hardly cares either, I think. I see only relief in his face. He's glad to have secured me in time to trade me away. He's giving orders, and people are moving quickly around us and I'm shoved into a pavilion with a very frustrated Lady Fliad. She speaks and when she doesn't get an intelligent answer from me, she strips us both, shoves a wet rag in my hands, and then grumbles when I do not clean myself well enough. She snatches the rag back, washes my face like I'm a child, and when she's done her own hurried washing she dresses us both in gowns of gold thread on blue – a strange design that must have come from the fae. They tighten with lacings at the back – a good thing since it means they can fit our drastically different figures – and then she runs a comb through our hair, dresses it hurriedly, and looks me over.

"I never thought you could put me in a position of a ladies' maid, Iva, and I'll never forgive you for doing this now. You've lost your senses, I swear."

She's practically spitting. I can't even focus on her

words. I just keep seeing him there, bleeding out in the woods, his eyes blank with death and it's like my mind can't hold other thoughts.

"This had better grant me favor with your father," she hisses in my ear, "or I will hunt you own, bride of the fae or not, and skin you alive."

I'm lucky to have her. In this, she is utterly practical where I am utterly useless.

And then she gives me a shove and we're out of the pavilion and being led to fresh horses, mounting them, and following my father the king, surrounded by grim men in his royal guard's red tabards, and riding hard out into what looks like a battlefield.

I gasp, my mouth falling open as we plunge between knots of fighting men. I keep seeing *him* wheeling his horse to save me. I bite back a scream when one of the royal guards stumbles and falls, an arrow meant for me stuck right through his neck. We don't even stop to help him, just keep riding at a full gallop toward a group of fae galloping from *their* front toward *us*.

They're led by a fae with pale hair that flows in the wind behind him, brushing his golden-winged helmet and gilt breastplate. He rides a white unicorn – really white, not a grey color like white horses often are, though it has muddy feet just like a mortal horse would – and he carries a sword with a hilt decorated with some kind of insect. Arrogance and pride are in his every movement.

And that's when I realize what is happening.

I'm about to get married in this silly gold and blue dress.

On a battlefield.

To that wicked-looking golden being.

And I look around me, wanting to panic, but all I see is the men falling and dying in this miserable mud field. And in every face I see, I keep seeing Haldur. If I don't do this, everything he fought for is lost. All the vassals he was trying to save are lost. If I care for him at all, then I need to give him the only thing he ever asked of me.

So, I steel my jaw, turn my eyes forward, and I ride.

22

IVA FITZROY

We meet in the middle and the fae fan out into a flower pattern with their king in the center. They all shine in the sun. Not one of them is less glorious than the next. They feel as if they are hardly part of this world. As if it almost is a desecration for one of them to marry me – a woman of mortal dust.

I expected us to dismount, but we don't. Our guards spread around us, guarding us both from those we are here to meet and those on the battlefield.

I glance behind me. Men are pouring forward in our wake, weapons brandished, as if our presence has thrown oil upon the flame. I spin back to look past the fae king, and see the same on his side. Far from bringing peace, we have brought more war. My belly twists. I watch as the fae behind him – the ones charging us – morph from beautiful warriors to terrible creatures of shadow and fire, high as trees as they charge toward our people and

I'm seeing them back in the forest, launching themselves toward us as I slip on poor Wildsage's blood.

I grit my teeth and hold my reins tightly, but the kings pay no attention to the battle even as a hail of arrows sails over us.

This is madness.

They are all fools.

"Hail Precatore, King of Iceheim," my father says, and I'm too distracted to hear the response.

Beside me, a horse stumbles, an arrow striking her in the neck. Her rider dismounts and my gaze is stuck on them, I can't help but think how unfair this is to the animals who never asked to be here, who are thrown into this violence with no care to their wants.

They are no different than the men, are they? Sir Oakensen doesn't want this. Gragor doesn't want this. None of them do, and yet here we are.

My wild eyes meet my father's as he introduces me, and then, to my surprise, the white unicorn steps forward, and Lady Fliad slips her hand onto my reins and guides my horse forward, too. I'm too stunned to do it. I meet her scornful eyes and she shakes her head minutely. If she were the one being wed there would be none of this slowness or balking.

A harried-looking counselor who someone calls "Lord Beecher" dismounts and hurries to a place between our horses and he grabs my hand with little care, jamming it against the ice-cold hand of the fae king and twisting both hands in a ribbon. That's not how we marry in our lands. It must be a fae custom.

As the ribbon begins to wind, the fae king's eyes meet

mine and now I can't look away – not out of admiration or longing as it had been with Haldur, but in the way that prey cannot look away from the predator.

I swallow.

"Speak the words of the prophecy," Precatore, King of Iceheim orders, and my mouth opens before I realize it's not me that he is ordering.

From beside us, one of the fae mounted on an elk intones the words in a voice like a bell.

"The Golden Prince a bride must take,
A mortal crowned for amity's sake,
She who nearly usurped the place,
Of her with greater royal grace.
Thus, bloodshed ends in solemn vow,
We kneel as one in common bow."

He pauses and my father breaks in, "We've brought her to you, now marry her quickly, and let this be done."

My terrifying groom lifts an eyebrow, but he does not disagree, instead, his beautiful mouth turns into a cruel, disdainful smile and he looks down at me and says, "Thus I marry thee, mortal girl – bastard daughter of this weak king. May this union bear the fruit of peace."

My lips are parted but no words come until Lady Fliad prods me in the ribs and I say, "Thus I marry thee, Precatore, King of Iceheim. May this union bear the fruit of peace."

He nods and he seems satisfied.

I feel only cold. Cold as if I were dead. Perhaps I am. They will bear me away now, to live in their icy halls, bereft of human friends and mortal animals, away from hearth and kindness. And I will never see Haldur again.

I swallow, and Precatore rips the ribbon from our hands roughly – a sign, I think, of how he will treat me. He casts it to the mud below, a look of triumph on his face. He reaches out and before I can gasp, he has plucked me from the back of my horse and set me before him on his snorting unicorn. I am not a heavy woman, but to him, I weigh less than a leaf in the wind.

My gaze swings back to my grim father and his court, still mounted, to Lady Fliad who looks wistful, her eyes fixed on Precatore as though she has seen her first rainbow.

And behind them, pounding across the battlefield, I see a horse with a wild rider on his back, hunched forward, low over the withers. He's too far away to know who he is.

And yet, I know.

He is alive.

And this is a last gift to me. A last glimpse of him. Maybe I will watch as peace settles over the field, the peace he bought with his heart. I find myself almost smiling even as my eyes prick with tears. I will have this last image of him to hold in my heart.

Our unicorn begins to turn. Precatore grasps my leg with a stone grip, holding me in place. My future awaits.

I'm surprised when he freezes, looks over my shoulder and his face goes dark. His unicorn dances nervously as we turn back to face my father.

"Treachery!" Precatore roars. "Think you to deceive *me?*"

23

HALDUR OAKENSEN

My breath saws in my lungs. I have not dared to stop. It came to me while I was fighting – an answer I had not considered.

The horse I borrowed thunders over the ground and my teeth rattle as I ride. I expect him to trip at any moment and send us both careening into the soldiers scattering before us. I should not be riding like this. Who knows who might sprain an ankle trying to get clear of my path, or slice a hand on a sword as they draw back from my rampage? But I dare not stop. I dare not arrive too late.

I grit my teeth and I ride faster.

I can see them up ahead, surrounded by a ring of soldiers as the fighting still rages all around. I maneuver sharply around Sir Gunthard and his vassals, and he shakes his fist at me in censure. If I survive this, I will owe him an apology at the very least.

Both fronts are colliding in the biggest battle I've seen in months. Usually, we harry the lines or pitch smaller battles, but for no reason that I can grasp, both armies have surged forward today as if to spill as much blood as possible before peace is forged – or maybe they never believed peace was possible. Maybe, to them, this is a last, desperate charge.

I'm drawing close enough to see individual faces in little glimpses between the world rising and falling under my horse's rough gait. I catch the merest glimpse of Iva, pale and terrified on Precatore's horse with him. We dip and rise, and my next glimpse is of Precatore, mouth open wide, eyes furious.

Something has gone wrong.

And I think I know what it is.

My borrowed horse is blowing unhappily, slick with sweat. I've treated him hard today. He does not deserve this. But we are almost there. Almost where he can rest, and I can try to save a peace treaty about to fracture into a thousand pieces.

My king gestures emphatically, a claim of innocence, I think. There is confusion in his gesticulating.

They are both posing as innocent parties. But I don't see either of them calling off the fighting. I don't see either of them asking for peace.

I pull my gasping horse up short in front of the ring of royal guard surrounding our king. One of them levels his lance at me but I brush the tip impatiently aside and dismount, leaving my poor stallion to huff and gasp and try to catch his breath from our pell-mell ride.

I need to watch my feet. The ground is uneven and there are wounded men stretched out between the nervous horses – a terrible oversight.

I lean in close to the man with the lance, point at his fellow gasping on the ground with an arrow in his thigh, and give him a pointed look. I have no authority here, but leaving their wounded like this is madness, and he should know it.

I'm too angry to care that I have exceeded my authority, but I don't dare take more time than that.

My eyes are searching. They meet her terrified gaze. Her bridegroom has his hand clenched on either of her shoulders and I see the lines of pain in her face at his rough grip.

Fire flares hot in my chest, but I dare not allow it to lick up to my tongue. If I cannot stay cool, I will make this worse, and it will be her who is dashed upon the rocks I so carefully step around.

"The curse has not lifted as the prophecy said it would!" Precatore snarls. "You've sold me a worthless bride."

"*What* curse?" my king throws back. Spittle flies with his words. "*What curse?*"

"The curse that turns your men to demons the moment we attack them." Precatore's voice is low and hateful. "The curse that makes them taller than walking trees with mouths of fire and bodies that swell and wane like pillars of smoke."

I feel my eyes widening and my jaw go slack as I see the same in every mortal man around me.

"But ... but that's what your kind does," Randalfur, the captain of the Royal Guard, says, and then closes his mouth hard. He didn't mean to speak. That's what you get for not keeping your words down tight.

"*Our* kind?" Precatore clutches the pommel of his sword as if he might draw it, but at least that means one hand has left Iva's shoulders. "You must be mad, for it is you mortals who have cursed us somehow, blinding our eyes to your true forms when you engage in war-play against us."

"There's nothing about war that's play," my king snarls and Prectore waves a hand dismissively.

"We want it gone. We want the curse lifted. It's why we are willing to agree to peace. Why I'm willing to take this husk of a bride to my home and bed."

I'm shaking so hard that I'm surprised my teeth don't rattle.

"But you've sold me a bucket with a hole in the bottom," Precatore says, leaning forward and seizing a handful of Iva's hair right at the scalp. He lifts her from the horse and her teeth clench in pain as her hands fly up to grip his arm, desperately trying to relieve the pressure from her hair. "You've deceived me and tricked me and …"

He doesn't get farther than that, though I'm sure there was more.

I've crossed the remaining ground without realizing it, leapt nimbly up, my foot finding purchase on his own where it sits in the stirrup, grabbed his forearm, and lowered his arm to take the tension off of Iva.

His eyes snap to mine as he tries to shake off my grip.

"You pay for this," he says. "Your hands have touched your better."

"So have yours," I say mildly.

I don't care that he is insulted. He's said there will be

no peace. No peace for us means no Iva for him. He can't keep only one half of his dread bargain. But perhaps he needs this situation explained to him.

"You married the wrong woman," I say simply. And I mean that in many ways, even if he can only grasp one of them.

"What?" his eyes flick from mine to my king's.

I don't waver. I keep my gaze level and firm as I lower myself to ground, removing my hand from his forearm.

He lets go of Iva's hair and she slumps down and to my surprise, slips from the unicorn's side and to her feet on the ground. He hasn't stopped her. She's watching me as everyone is now, I realize.

I'm going to have to speak, and I'm not very good at speaking. I swallow twice, my mouth too dry to get the words out. I have eyes only for her.

Which is why I can see it when understanding dawns in her face. Her eyes go wide. She looks at her father and then her bridegroom and then at me again.

My mouth works again, and this time I manage the words.

"*She who nearly usurped the place, Of her with greater royal grace.* That's the prophecy. It doesn't refer to birth. It speaks to action. Lady Fliad tried to take Lady Iva's place along the journey here."

That's the best I can manage.

"Is this true?" my king asks over my head.

I hear Lady Fliad confirming it, but I have eyes only for Iva. Her face is wet with tears, but there's something in her eyes I haven't seen before, and I can't look away from them. It's like she sees peace in my face.

"Then annul this sham marriage and let us proceed with the prophesied bride, or is it your intention to trick the trickster?" the fae king is asking, and I realize he must be truly as desperate as we are to have condescended to marry a mortal and now stand here in the mud and debate which one it is to be.

I step back, and I feel my face flaming. My purpose here has been met and it's not for me to stay and to watch. Among all present, my place is lowest. I turn my gaze down, wrenching it from Iva's. It's not my place to stay with her, though I wish I could. She's the daughter of the king. She should be honored by him and surely, she will be when these speeches have passed.

I find my horse as I hear Lord Beecher speaking the words of severance over Iva and Precatore, King of Iceheim, and then the words of binding over Lady Fliad and the king who is now her groom.

I peek over my shoulder then, just in time to see a glow surround them, and then Precatore sighs, and the sigh runs all down the line of men and fae. We all freeze. No one needs to tell me that peace has come. I see it in the postures of both armies. I see it in the slumped shoulders of the nearest royal guard.

I want to weep with it.

I feel like a lost child.

I stand there for three full breaths, staring at the ground. Trying to control the flood of emotion washing over me.

When, at last, I have mastered it, I make my way to my horse, not knowing what comes next or where to go.

To my vassals, I suppose, those who remain. To the burial of those who do not.

I try not to let that make me feel hollow.

Behind me, the wedding is concluding, orders are being given, solemn vows made. We will break camp and withdraw – both armies will – as a sign of good faith.

The war is over.

And everyone has what they want – or so the kings are saying, and so I'm sure Lady Fliad agrees.

I have done my part. And it's no one's fault but mine if I shattered my own heart while doing it.

I reach the horse's head and rub his forelock, my eyes still downcast. He's recovering from the run, but I'll have to be gentle with him now. He can't be pushed faster than a walk.

I lean my head against his. I have this terrible, cracked feeling as if I might break in two if I look up. As if everyone will see then that I've bought what I came to buy and it's nothing but ashes in my hands.

I reach the stirrup, meaning to mount, but there's a boot in it.

And I can't keep looking down if I want to know who is taking my horse, so I look up.

I'm not a man who weeps. Or at least, I am not supposed to be.

Iva is sitting in my saddle. She's smiling gently in that way she does.

I don't know how she slipped away even faster than I did. I don't care. I barely dare to breathe. What if I exhale too forcefully and she blows away like mist?

She kicks her boot from the stirrup and offers me a hand and I freeze in place.

"I'm riding with you," she says simply. "You have more holes in your coat and they need mending."

I look down stupidly. I do have holes. Slashes. A bloodstain.

"Unless that's not what you want?" she sounds timid suddenly and there's to be none of that.

I launch myself into the saddle behind her, wrap an arm around her waist possessively, and whisper in her ear, only for her.

"Come away from this place, and be my bride, and we two shall know true peace."

She wiggles in my embrace enough to face me, sending tiny thrills through me from my abdomen to the tips of my ears, and she smiles that devastating smile, and she doesn't say anything. She just lets me look into those eyes full of hope and home and all the things I keep tight by my spine loosen, and I feel like I'm taking a breath for the first time. It's a breath full of Iva and I want to breathe nothing else forever.

EPILOGUE

HALDUR OAKENSEN

I stand by the edge of the lake and listen to the sound of the reeds in the wind, of the water lapping against the bank, of our horses cropping grass. A duck lands in a flurry of wings and water and I am at peace. I let the air into my lungs. It lingers there before I release it again. I let the wind flow through my hair and tangle my cloak.

Far away, up the hill, is Castle Tor. We're rebuilding the walls and rethatching the roof and cleaning the brambles in the garden. We're fixing all the things that fell into disrepair while the men were gone and the women held on grimly to keep for us what little they could.

I've brought home just twenty vassals. The five who survived the journey to retrieve Iva and Fliad, and the fifteen who survived waiting for us with the main army. So very few. Too few.

But we will rebuild, and we will sow peace into our fields, and build faithfulness into our walls, and bake love into our bread. I breathe in hope with every breath, and it feels too good, too sweet, as if it might be gone in a moment.

I press my eyes tightly closed in this stolen moment away from it all and I try to tell myself it's here to stay, even if that's impossible to believe.

Warm arms wrap around me and a slight body presses against mine. My lips are turning up into a smile even before my arms respond to draw her close and to lean my cheek onto the top of her hair. She is home. She makes any place I go a home – from a grim campfire in the snow, to this ancestral house of mine.

I married her without asking her father. If he doesn't like it, he can come to me and make war.

But I know he will not. There are many things he will not wish to remember about the Fae War. One of them being how willing he was to sell his own daughter to a fae king. Or how near he came to failing even at that. I think he'll ignore us if we stay far away from court. And if he does not, then I will fight to defend her. I have before. I will forever.

There is only one sadness left to mar all this joy. I try not to think about it too often, but it hides, still, next to my spine, tangling up around me and choking me sometimes in hours when I ought to be happy.

Iva helps to mend that, but I'm not sure anyone can mend it fully. I'm not sure that they should.

Iva stiffens in my arms suddenly, and my eyes blink open, worried.

I look down at her and she looks up with an expression so full of joy that it stabs like a spear to the side. I still can't believe she's mine. She carries with her such sweet draughts of kindness, as if her very presence heals poisonous vapors and wounds of the heart. I find myself drifting to her side whenever I am not occupied with work, just to be near that font of healing.

"Haldur," she says, pressing a hand to my cheek.

I sigh happily at the feel of it and the sound of my name on her sweet tongue.

"Haldur," she repeats, and her smile broadens, if that is possible. "Look."

I have to tear my gaze from hers to follow her pointing finger and when I do, my heart goes cold. But it's not the cold of fear.

Chills wash over me. I fall to my knees, barely able to breathe, barely able to think.

And then weight crashes into my chest and I'm clutching dark fur to me as my face is washed and washed again by a doggy tongue, and I think I might be crying, but I don't know if I am. Can a heart break from happiness? I suppose I will find out now that Hessa is back.

And if the knight who stole her comes looking for her, well, I'll make war on him, too.

The last thing uncoils from around my spine.

Peace is here.

Home is here.

And I am free.

ABOUT THE SERIES:

Arranged Marriages of the Fae is a multi-author series of short novels written by seven romantic fantasy authors on the same theme. These books can be read on their own, but you'll have so much more fun if you read the whole series!

As authors, we want to thank you for getting swept away by our fantasy romances and we wish you hours of enjoyment and escape!

XOXO

***

Married by Wind
Married by Fate
Married by Scandal
Married by War
Married by Treachery
Married by Starfall
Married by Dusk

FIND THEM ALL HERE

***

Or, choose your next read by trope!

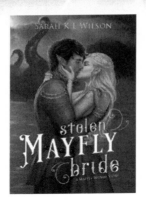

S ometimes stealing a life is the only way to save it.

Elkhana is the Mayfly Seer. Ripped from her family, drowned, and set into a magical cage, she lives only one day a year to tell fortunes for her former people. When Vidar meets her, he sees a resource he can use to save himself from his enemies and the torturous demands of his own liege and court.

But the bond between Elkhana and Vidar is growing.

She's slipping into his dreams and changing how he sees the world and he doesn't know if he can keep on using her now that he sees her as a person. Without her visions, he's powerless against his enemies, but if he has the chance to steal her away from her cage, shouldn't he take it?

To succeed, he'll need a plan, a lot of nerve, and all the bargains he can strike. Will it be enough?

STOLEN MAYFLY BRIDE is a stand-alone fantasy romance perfect for fans of Elise Kova or Laini Taylor.

.

Made in the USA
Middletown, DE
03 December 2022

16927348R00080